THE SINS OF SEVEN SERIES

INDULGE

DANI RENÉ

Published by Dani René

Second Edition Print ISBN 978-1-8384492-1-6
eBook ISBN 978-0-6399366-0-4

The following story contains mature themes, strong language, and sexual situations. It is intended for adult readers.

WARNING

In a world of secrets, where sins are hidden from sight, people live their lives hoping that those around them never know what desires they conceal. The darkest needs, those that taunt just below the surface. Those they hide in the deepest recesses of their minds. Those things they don't admit to. The things they don't talk about. That's what this series touches on. You may find some of the subject matter disturbing, you may even look away, cringe, and gasp. But that's why I wanted to write these seven couples. These couples came to me with their confessions and I obeyed their need to have their stories told. The dark, depraved, the taboo. The things we may find tempting, alluring, and may even be turned on by it. That's what I wanted to write.

Each story is an interconnected standalone, delving into the relationship of the couples you'll meet. There will be sex, there will most certainly be foul language. And there will DEFINITELY be taboo subjects covered.

The Sins of Seven revolves around seven couples who are so different in nature, in what their likes and dislikes are. They're each unique in desire, in their personalities, and even in the way they try to show affection. They don't love. At least, they don't think they do, they don't believe they're worthy of it.

Each story will make a point of focusing on one of the seven deadly sins.

Greed, Pride, Lust, Gluttony, Sloth, Wrath, Envy.

Although they'll be released in their own order, you'll be able to tell which sin, follows which couple and their journey to possibly find their happily ever after.

Please heed this warning.

**This is a dark romance, suitable for mature audiences, 18+ ONLY. Strong sexual themes and violence, which could trigger emotional distress, are found in this story. Certain scenes are graphic and could be upsetting to some. Proceed with caution. Discretion is advised.*

"And I cannot trsut myself to

untangle your veins from mine."

R. Sternberg

To my ladies, my colleagues, my friends.

Don't be afraid to indulge.

Don't be afraid to take a chance.

Don't be afraid to submit.

Don't allow society to tell you what you want is wrong.

And never hide who you are.

Be strong.

Be you.

Love hard.

And live your life for you!

Prologue

Carrick

I've lived a life of indulgence. I don't remember a time I wanted for anything. I was a man who could have any woman on his arm, drive any car I wanted, and travel to the most exotic locations in the world anytime I pleased. Most would think that's what dreams are made of, and for a long time, so did I.

That was until the inevitable happened. When all I had was cruelly ripped out of my hands. At the age of twenty-eight, I walked out and left my home, my family, and everything I knew to move to America. An Englishman in a country where I was a stranger. I was no longer the man who was feared; I was a man people wanted to know.

With my finances intact, I approached an old friend, Mason, and we opened Seven Sins together. I poured everything into a place where people don't have to hide who they are. Where I don't have to hide who I really am. Now, at thirty-six, I have a life most men my age can only dream of.

Only . . . I hide so much more than anyone knows.

"Mr. Anderson." Her voice comes from the sofa, and I cast her a glance. She's a new performer I'm thinking of hiring. A contortionist who will be working with one of the Dom's to perform positions with rope. Mason and Savvie are planning a vacation, and I want someone who's going to keep my customers interested.

"Do you take orders?" She nods. Her face is sweet, pretty even. Her long, black hair hangs to the middle of her back. She's got big, brown eyes that are slanted, hinting at her Asian genes. "Get on your knees," I tell her, watching her move to the floor where I've pointed. My office is decked out in beautiful implements to use on the submissives who dare walk in here.

I'm not a sadist by any means, but I do enjoy showing a woman how little control she has when I'm near. I can make a woman come just by taunting her nipples and clit. But that's not my kink. I'm a man who enjoys indulgence. Multiple women worshiping my cock is what I enjoy. I no longer want love or to own just one submissive. I train them, I make them ache for me, then I shove them into the arms of another Dominant. Never get attached. Don't let emotion in. And never, never take a submissive more than once.

I've learned that the love of a sub is something you cannot ever counter. They love hard. They give their all, and that's something to be very wary of. I have rules. Five to be exact. And I've never deviated from them. This is how I've become the man that every woman that walks into my club wants. They all crave to kneel before me.

"Open your mouth and stick your tongue out. You're going to swallow my cock. If you can do so without puking, you've got the job." She obeys without question. "I'm going to fuck your pretty face, and when I'm done, you'll leave. If I give you the job, you'll return tomorrow evening at seven. Am I understood?"

"Yes, Mr. Anderson." Beautiful. Rising, I stalk toward her while unzipping my slacks.

"Good girl."

Her big eyes peek up at me as I fist my cock. It's hard, ready to see what she's made of. As I slide into her mouth, I forget. My mind blanks out the pain, the agony, and the ache I live with daily. It's the only time I am able to shove the memories away, when I'm inside a woman.

I forget who I was.

I forget what I did.

And with each cunt I fuck, mouth I use, and ass I drive my cock into, I become a new man. One no longer needy for love. No. I create an animal. Hungry and feral. A man no woman will love. Because I'm not deserving of it. Never have been, and never will be.

One

Carrick

Buttoning up my charcoal suit jacket over the crisp white dress shirt, I make my way from my office down the long dimly lit hallway. Tonight is the VIP gala event where we invite esteemed guests dressed in the most expensive designer gowns and suits to scope out Seven Sins.

When I reach the staircase, Mason, my partner and best friend, strolls up beside me.

"You have a list of women waiting for you," he tells me in a low, warning tone.

It's the same each night. I have women at my beck and call. They all want to spend one sinful night with me. There's no room in my life for a full-time submissive, but I partake in the delicacies they have on offer, then send them on their way to find another Dominant who can collar them. I love to indulge, being a glutton for sweet moans and delicious whimpers, and most of all, feeling the tight pulsing heat of a wet cunt.

"I take it you'll be with Savvie on stage for the evening?" I question, not responding to his earlier comment. The club is decked in silver, gold, and black. The furniture is jet faux leather, with delicate silk fabric that hangs from ceiling to floor in the softest shade of pink. The silver tables, along with the bar, offsets the luxurious feel of our club.

"I might take her into one of the rooms as well. Perhaps train one of the other submissives who asked for a female and female pairing," he tells me as we make our way to the bar. Savannah is Mason's beautiful blonde submissive. They've been together for far longer than I care to imagine, but for some reason, he's never married her. Granted, being collared means more in this life, but there are times I see how she looks at him. It's no secret, Savvie wants a ring.

Dylan smiles from the other side of the bar when we reach it. "Good evening, gentlemen," he says in his boyish tone. Oliver would have a field day with him.

But I heard the man has taken on a new slave who's been on the waiting list for a couple weeks. Yes, Oliver Michaelson has a waiting list of newbies wanting to experience the lifestyle. I can't wait to hear the feedback from that pairing.

"D, can you get me a gin and tonic, single," I tell him. Mason orders his normal brandy on ice, while I perch on one of the stools. Each time someone enters the club, my attention is dragged to the door. I'm not sure what I'm looking for, but none of the women in the club at this particular moment grab my attention.

Three women sidle in at that moment, all of them giggling like teenagers. Easy pickings. Yeah, I'm an asshole. There wasn't a day in my life I denied it. And when a quick, easy fuck presents itself, I don't deny my need. I pick up the tumbler that's been set before me and take a sip while keeping my gaze trained on them. Perhaps I'm a glutton, but having three women worshiping me for the night sounds like a plan.

"I'll see you later, Mase," I tell my best friend and head toward the booth the women have chosen. "Ladies," I murmur, stopping at their table. All three snap their gazes toward me—blue, brown, and green.

"Hello," *blue eyes* mumbles shyly.

"Are you ladies here for the show? Or are you looking for something more . . . particular?" I ask, lifting my glass to my lips, while meeting each set of eyes for a moment, lingering on them. Making eye contact with a woman is a sure-fire way to get into those pretty knickers they wear.

Brown eyes smiles. "We're actually here looking for . . . well . . . we were told that Carrick Anderson is one of the most sought-after Dominants in the club. Beside the fact that he owns the place. We just wanted to experience a scene with him."

"I see." I nod, quickly glancing at the bar, signaling Dylan. Once he reaches us, I look at the ladies once more and offer a nod. "Dylan will sort you out with the confidentiality agreement. He will bring you one drink. Nothing more. If I'm going to have three submissives under my care tonight, I want them of sound mind."

"You're . . .?" *blue eyes* gasps.

"The one and only. Nice to meet you, ladies. I'll be seeing you in about twenty minutes." I tip my head in greeting and walk away. Dylan knows exactly what I need and want. Every woman who walks into a scene with me signs an agreement. She is to understand there are safe words which she can use at her discretion. She will also be told how to be kneeling when I enter the room, and under no circumstance is she supposed to be high or heavily intoxicated.

"Three?" Mason says when I reach him once more. "You're slipping there, Rick. I would've easily thought you could handle more." He chuckles.

"I may be a glutton, Mase, but I'm not greedy." I wink, slapping his back as I head down toward the back rooms of the club.

Whenever I decide to play a scene, there's one room that's mine and only mine. It's draped in black satin and silk the color of graphite. The sofas are velvet. A St. Andrews Cross sits against one wall with leather cuffs for both wrists and ankles. A spanking bench along with some beautifully intricate toys to torture my slaves with hanging on one wall. There's a small changing room with restroom for the subs to use after we're done.

Even though my office is my haven, this room is for

when I take on multiple subs at a time. Upon entering, I make my way to the wall, pulling off the two whips, along with a flogger I might use. I proceed in setting out the rest of the toys, opening two new butt plugs along with lube. I don't know their experience, but from their pretty doe-eyes peering at me like lambs about to head to the slaughter, I'd say they're fairly new to this.

Moments later, the door opens, and Dylan escorts three beautiful toys into the room. They're dressed in silk robes, bare feet, and each one with her hair in a ponytail.

"Thank you, Dylan. That's all," I tell him. Once he's gone, I don't speak. They move silently as they've been instructed and drop the robes. Once they're naked apart from tiny black panties, all three kneel with their hands behind their back, causing their tits to jut out.

I watch them intently as I unbutton my jacket, shrugging it off and hanging it on the rack in the far corner. My shirt is off in moments, and I'm left with my slacks and socks on.

"Do you understand why you're kneeling?" I ask, my tone commanding and dominant.

"Yes, Sir," they respond in unison. My cock jolts at

their reaction.

"And you remember your safe words?"

"Red, Yellow, and Green." Once again, they respond beautifully.

I make my way over to the implements I set out and pick up a small leather crop. Stalking toward my sub toys, I lift the implement and gently stroke it over each of their thighs. Gentle trembles trail through them at the touch of the cool material.

"Eyes up," I command, and they each lift their gazes to me. "One by one, I want you to tell me your names," I command them. My confident demeanor emanates from me like a cologne. I'm in charge of three sexy women who are about to do anything I tell them.

More than eight years of torturing willing women—subs, slaves, toys, pets, whatever they're called—has hardened me. It's changed me. There's pleasure, pain, but no emotion. That part of me closed off a long time ago.

"Monica," says *blue eyes*. Lifting the crop, I bring it down on her bare tit, causing her to yelp.

"I trust you know how to address me?" I hiss,

leaning in, meeting her gaze with one of my own serious glares.

"Monica, Sir." Her voice is melodic, with a tremble of fear trickling through it.

I turn to *brown eyes*, and she responds easily. "Jenna, Sir." My gaze shifts over her, and I nod. When my eyes fall on the last girl, green eyes pierce me. "Alicia, Sir." Rising to full height, I take them each in. Monica is beautiful, her curves are soft, her tits large with dark brown nipples. Jenna is slim, smaller than her friend, but she has the most incredible set of tits, a handful with rosy nipples. When I glance at Alicia once more, I can't help taking in the ink that adorns her toned, almost athletic body. She could be a gymnast with her build. All three incredibly beautiful, yet so different.

"Good girls. Stand. All three of you." They rise easily, and I head toward the large queen-sized bed. Shoving my slacks down, I step out of them, along with my socks. The briefs I'm wearing leave very little to the imagination. "I want you, Jenna, on the bed." She moves quickly, her hips swaying as she lies back. I proceed to bind her wrists and ankles while the other two watch in awe.

"Alicia, you'll be kneeling between her thighs." My orders are swift as the little toy moves in position. "And you, pet, will be sitting on her face, without those panties on."

The blush that spreads across her cheeks is enough to tell me she's never done anything this naughty before. But she doesn't respond, she merely moves toward her friend and straddles her face.

The tiny thong Jenna is wearing, I reach for it and rip it from her hips. "Get to work," I tell Alicia as she gasps at me. Tentatively, they move in sync while I lift the crop, bringing it down on Jenna's exposed tits, stomach, and her legs.

Moans echo through the room along with whimpers of pleasure as I watch the three slaves writhe in gratification. I palm my dick in my boxers while I rain down swats on all three girls. As the rapture heightens, they move faster, losing themselves in the ecstasy of the moment. Small red prints mark their pale flesh, and I smirk in satisfaction.

"Stop." All three women ceases movement

immediately. "Which one of you wanted pain?"

Alicia's beautiful eyes sparkle. "I did." I move, undoing the restraints, allowing Jenna and Monica to watch as I take their little friend and have her stand before me. I grab the clamps and lean in, suckling on each of her tiny nipples. They harden for me, and I proceed in clamping them with the metal teeth. She whimpers as the pain sears through her.

"At the cross," I order, and she shuffles toward the wooden X against the wall, the chains of her clamps clinking in the silence of the room. Once she's bound, I grab my flogger. Turning to the other two girls, I tell them, "I want you both in a sixty-nine, right now." They obey dutifully. Lifting the flogger, I swat Alicia along her stomach. She cries out, and my cock hardens further. I lash her again and again. Her body trembling in the leather cuffs. She can't move. Tears stream from her eyes, but she doesn't call *red*.

"Please, Sir," she pleads then, her eyes glistening like jewels.

"What? Tell me what you want?" I ask. Her gaze falls to her friends who are in a frenzy on the bed, wet slurping sounds that make my dick needy.

"The cane." Her words jar me, and I stare at her for a moment.

Shaking my head, I respond, "I don't use the cane." Her face falls at my words, but I can't bring myself to pick the offending item up. Ever. I reach for my belt on the floor and fold it in half. "You'll get leather instead." I don't wait. I lift it easily, bringing it down onto her thighs in a harsh *thwack*. I continue marking her. The pleasure from doling it out is enough to keep me high for days. When I finally drop the belt, her legs are full of angry red welts. She wanted this. I'm a monster, but I can't help it. This is who I am.

I unbind her and lead her to the bed. The other two pets are curled around each other, their mouths busily feasting on the other. "Enough," I order in a gruff tone. My cock is throbbing painfully. I don't offer Alicia anything more than a smile after whipping her.

It's not that I don't care, but once I'm done, Dylan will come in and offer them the calm they need after a scene. Like I said, no emotion. They move off each other, and I settle on the bed, pulling a small foil packet from the nightstand and sheath myself. I'm lying on my back and gesture for Alicia to straddle my cock. Monica is between my thighs. Her wet tongue lapping at my balls and licking her friend's asshole. I watch the scene for a moment, reveling in the filthy little sluts that are here for me.

"On my face," I say, pointing at Jenna. She obeys without questions as she straddles me, her smooth, drenched cunt at my mouth as I suck on her clit. Her hips buck, her cries otherworldly as I roughly shove two fingers inside her hole.

The four of us move, fuck, and lick in that position. All I hear are the moans, the mewls of three wanton whores who love my dick. Alicia's tight pussy pulses around my erection, and her body locks while Jenna's delicious juices drip down my chin. I'm still hard when I shift a trembling Jenna and Alicia off me.

"Monica, pull that rubber off and show me how much you love my dick. Put that sweet fuck hole of yours on my face." The command is easy, and the little minx positions herself as a six, and I'm her nine. Her mouth envelops me all the way to the base. Her gagging sounds spur me on, and I devour her cunt, my tongue darting into her like I would fuck her with my cock. Her hips roll as she rides my face, and my hips lift as I plunge into her throat. Each time I do, her heat tightens around my three fingers, and I bite down on her clit causing her to scream around my dick, and I can't hold off my orgasm anymore. Shooting hot spurts down her throat, I revel in the filthy indulgence of my life.

Two

Peyton

"Pey, you don't have to leave, you know?" My brother sounds so sad. Chance Moore has been there all my life, literally. My twin brother who always teases me that he was the one born with all the looks and I got the brains.

My rock.

As much as I want to stay, I need to do this. It's been a long while since I've done something for myself. And with Michael, my ex-fiancé, locked up for what he did, I can finally move on.

My past is ugly. The pain I've lived with for so long has held me back, shoved me into the darkest of depressions. I can't trust anyone. Only Chance. But no more. I'll never allow my fear of living hold me back.

My parents were always forceful in telling us what we had to do rather than nurturing us. But then again, my father had his dodgy dealings to worry about. With his connection to the mob here in New York, he thought he'd make it out alive, but the night he and Mom were killed ensured that Chance and I were orphans before we hit twenty-one.

"Listen to me," Chance implores, and I drag my gaze to him. "He was wrong for you, we all know that, but he's paying for what he did, and he'll never hurt you." He tells me something I knew anyway. With a life sentence without the chance of parole, I know Michael can't hurt me, but deep down, I feel like I need to finally spread my wings. "You, running away, that is not what Mom and Dad would've wanted." The mention of my parents only solidifies my choice.

When Savannah called me up and told me to spend time with her in Chicago, I jumped at the chance. Her boyfriend, Mason, owns a club there; but I know she's into the BDSM lifestyle, and something about hearing her stories makes me want to see what the fuss is about.

When I told her I wanted to try, she agreed to help

me through my journey to find out what I want. When she told me there's no strings at the club and I can walk away at any time, I booked my flight.

"You'll make an awesome lawyer one day, arguing your cases, but I need to do this. I spent two years mourning our parents and what that asshole did to me. I can't do it anymore, Chance."

He sighs, his green eyes that match mine shimmer with emotion. "Fine. But if you find me some hot man, I'll forgive you for leaving me." He chuckles.

My brother has loved and lost. He knows how broken I feel. Learning the man that you love is a murderer does wonders for your self-confidence. I was blinded. So were my parents. But now, choosing someone to be with, let alone start a relationship with, is becoming a task I'd rather not embark on.

I was engaged to Michael since I was eighteen. For years, he doted on me, on my family, but when the truth finally came to light, I watched him get cuffed and lose his plea for freedom in court. Even now, nightmares haunt me of hearing those metal gates shutting him inside and me on the other.

"And don't you worry your pretty little head about me, chicken. I'll not be alone for too long," he teases, shoving my suitcase closed with a loud whoosh.

"You need to stop falling for every pretty boy you see," I tease, throwing a pillow at his face. He's been lying on my bed, his hand holding up his head watching me pack.

"Then find me some hot, older guy, and I'll kneel for him," he tells me with a wicked grin on his face. He's handsome, with blonde hair and green eyes, and a smile that can have any woman falling for him. I was convinced my brother was gay; then he told me he's bi. He loves both sides of the coin. I love how free he is about his sexuality, while I've only dated Michael, and the worst of it is, I'm still a damn virgin.

Daddy wanted me to be with Michael because *he had a good head on his shoulders*. It was utter bull crap. He was only doing what he could to get into my family's money.

"You know, I have no idea what I'm getting into," I confess, flopping on the bed beside him. Staring up at the ceiling, I play scenarios in my head. All the while I've been with Michael, it was what Savvie calls *vanilla.* The word alone sounds boring. Michael and I would make out, he'd touch me, and then he'd let me make him hard with my mouth. Other than that, he never took the next step to make love to me.

"Pey, if there's any advice I can give, it's that you need to start living. Feel rather than think. Perhaps you should just indulge while you're there."

I turn my head to face him. My twin brother. "So, you want me to turn into a slut?" I giggle, rolling my eyes.

"Hey, if that will get that stick out from up your ass, I'm all for it." He goads me into another swift slap on his shoulder. "Hey!" We collapse in a fit of hysterics. I'll miss this. Miss him.

"What if I get there and I hate it?" The fear of trying something new causes anxiety to twist itself in my stomach, twirling itself around me like a vine of thorns.

"What if you get there and meet a handsome, successful Dominant who'll take you to new heights? And maybe even teach you a thing or two about having an *actual* orgasm?" Chance utters, and I know it's a dig at Michael.

All the years I was with my ex-fiancé, the only time I actually felt something remotely close to an orgasm was when I touched myself. Granted, my father wanted us together. He was thrown at me without so much as an explanation other than he'll be able to look after me. I didn't realize what it meant until I found out what Daddy really did behind closed doors.

But I wasn't what he was looking for. No, he needed the fortune my father had. Only, when my parents were gone, and he realized there wasn't a family inheritance, Michael turned sour. For days after the funeral, I wondered what happened to him, but then I overheard his conversation, and the truth struck me like a slap in the face.

Michael inadvertently killed my parents. All he ever wanted was the money, but there was nothing left. My dad owned his own company, and we lived in luxury all those years, but it wasn't because of profits. It was because of loans from dangerous men, and when Mom and Dad were gone, they came to collect. All Chance's and my so-called inheritance went to pay off debt. It was either that, or we work for them. There wasn't a chance that was happening.

My job as the PA to an event planner has just gone belly up, but thankfully I managed to put away enough money for a rainy day or ten. Chance has been lucky. He landed a job at an established law firm helping with research and earns enough to get by without me.

When I told him I wanted to go to Chicago to see Savvie, the following day, my brother gave me the keys for an apartment he told me is paid up for two months. Enough time for me to find a job when I get there and pay my own way.

"You'll find love, Pey. You know that, right?" He looks so serious, a genuine expression on his face.

"Don't start that, Chance," I tell him, pushing off the bed and pulling on my sweater. It's almost time to get to the airport, and since I'm flying from JFK, I need to leave soon to ensure I don't miss my flight.

"I'll come visit as soon as that goddamn man gives me time off," he grumbles. His boss works him too hard. Even him being here for an hour to say goodbye to me was a mission to achieve.

"I love you," I tell him, knowing he has to get back to work. His messy blonde hair is sticking up in all directions from being flopped on my bed.

"Look after yourself, Toots," he tells me with grin. When my brother pulls me into a hug, I can't stop the tears from burning my eyes. I don't want to cry. I know this isn't goodbye, but it feels so much like I'm leaving him, and that hurts. It's just been the two of us for so long that I don't remember a time I wasn't by his side, or vice versa.

"You too, little bro." I smile as he pulls away. His face is stoic as he steels his expression. Always the strong one.

"I love you, Pey. And don't let some asshole shove you around. If someone hurts you, I'll be on the next flight out. You hear me?" he tells me in that commanding yet loving tone. Even though I'm older by a few minutes, he's always been the more mature one. The rock.

"Don't make me cry. I'll call you when I get there."

He nods and leaves me to finish up.

Once I have everything packed, I lock up and head out to the cab waiting on the sidewalk. I don't have much, but the suitcase I do have is filled with clothes, photos of Chance and me, and a lot of hopes and dreams.

"I hope you'll enjoy your stay here, darling. If you need anything, you're welcome to let us know." The old lady who has shown me to my new home smiles up at me kindly.

I nod. "Thank you, this is lovely," I tell her, and it's true. She offers a grin before shutting the door behind her and leaving me in my new apartment. The immaculate space is comfortable enough for one person. Furnished with two simple yet comfortable sofas, an armchair, and a window seat, the colors are neutral, and I love that it's not overdone.

Living without luxury for so long has allowed me to get used to the normal middle-class life. There are no longer boutique stores I frequent, and Michelin-star restaurants are not the order of the day. But somehow, even without all the money we used to have, I find I'm happier. More at ease. I have nothing to prove to anyone.

I head straight for the bedroom, finding a lovely

king-sized bed flush against the wall opposite the entrance. To my left is a small vanity, and just beyond that is a window which has a small bench seat. To the right, I notice a closet. It's small, but it's a walk-in with shelves and hanging space enough for me.

I'm tired, and I know Savvie wanted to meet up. Perhaps I can put it off until tomorrow. She's been begging me to visit Sins, and even though I'm intrigued, I'm also nervous. Being with one man all my life has left me inexperienced. She mentioned a while ago she wanted to set me up with Mason's partner, Carrick, but something happened since we spoke last that's changed her mind. Of course, this has left me curious. And you know what they say about curiosity killing the cat.

I'm about to see if I can find some food when my phone rings.

"Hey girl," I answer with a smile.

"Pey, I'm so excited to see you. Are you coming by later, or did you want to spend a night relaxing before coming down to Sins?" She sounds so hopeful, I want to say yes, but I think I need time to settle in.

"Yeah, I think I need some time to get my bearings.

I'll be there tomorrow, Sav. I'm nervous," I confess to her on a sigh. I feel like a damn virgin. Scratch that, I am a virgin, unlike my best friend.

"Try not to be. You'll be fine. You won't be alone. Think about it, Pey. Many others have been where you are. I have as well. I'll introduce you to a few lovely Dominants. Get your toes dipped in the pool, so to speak. Also, you don't have to have sex. I know . . . I mean, being as innocent as you are, I want your first time to be special, and who knows? If you like someone, maybe you'll let go, and if not, then it's fine as well," she whispers conspiratorially.

"I know. I feel so out of my depth. What Dominant is going to want a virgin?" I huff. "I mean, I'm twenty-two. I'm old," I pout.

"You'll be very fucking surprised, darling. Don't put so much pressure on yourself. Just let things happen. Everything will fall into place, and if you're not enjoying yourself, you can say no."

Sighing, I settle on the bed, staring up at the ceiling. I know she's right. There's nothing more I want than to experience sex, passion, that hunger I see between

Savvie and Mason.

"I'm seriously only considering this since you've suggested it," I tell her, and I can't help grinning at her excited giggle.

"Sure you are," her response comes, and I know she's probably more excited than I am. "Listen to your heart. If you feel you want to do a scene, then I'll set it up. If not, we can get drunk, and you can ogle all the men who walk in here every night." She makes it sound so easy. "I know it's difficult, but if you never try, you'll never know. What if you find out you love it? Listen to me, Peyton, this is not for everyone, I know that, but deep down, all I want is for you to be happy. You could have a scene with one of the experienced Doms. I'll tell him you're new, and you're just wanting to try it out. And I'll be close by if you need anything."

"I know. Thank you for doing this, darling. I've been stuck in that goddamn rut for so long, when Michael finally got put away, when my sadness took over, I just gave up for too long. I was angry, and now all I need is to not think so much. Chance has been a sweetheart putting up with me, but it's time for me to sort my life out."

Savannah sighs. "You just need to move the fuck on from that asshole. He used you all those years. He made you believe in a lie. Not all men are like that, babe. And don't even get me started on his fucking job," she bites out angrily. "You deserve someone who's going to care for you. Who can be there for you no matter what happens in your life."

"You're right." I flop back onto the bed.

"I'm always right, Pey," she responds sassily.

"Does Mason agree with that statement?" I tease, giggling when she grunts into the phone.

I've spent time around them, and I must be honest. I'm jealous over how much he dotes on her. She's his everything. I want that. I would give anything to have a man look at me the way Mason looks at Savvie.

"He'll agree to anything at this stage. I've told him I've gotten us tickets to the Rome Bondage Fair. He's been wanting to go for years. Carrick has agreed that he'll be here to look after the club while we're gone."

At the mention of Carrick, I recall Savvie's spoken about Mason's partner in the club a few times, even mentioned she'd set me up with him, but apparently, he's an asshole who plays the field. I've only ever seen photos of him, and I must be honest. He's definitely sexy. He has a suave aura about him. Dresses in immaculate suits. Brown hair that glints with hints of gold, which sits messily atop his head. He's got sharp features, with a prominent jaw and full lips that make me want to feel them against mine in a hungry kiss. And those goddamn eyes. Gold with flecks of green and brown.

"Are you listening to me, Pey?" My best friend's voice comes from the other end of the line, dragging me from thoughts of Carrick Anderson.

"Yeah, sorry. Uhm . . . No, what did you say?"

"You get some rest, and we'll talk tomorrow. I'll be here at six, so don't be late," she informs me sternly. She's always been like an older sister to me. Between her and Chance, I don't know how I would've made it through the heartbreak of Michael.

"Thanks again, love," I tell her.

Once I hang up, I head to the bathroom. I need a shower and sleep. And tomorrow will be the first day of my new life. Maybe I can talk Mason and Carrick into giving me a job. Who knows?

THREE

CARRICK

My phone ringing drags me from a heavy sleep, dreaming of a time when things were easier. But when I glance at the screen, I know as much as I've run away from that life, it's never let me go. Swiping my finger over the screen, I press the phone to my ear only to hear my brother's voice. "Rick."

"Callan." I utter my brother's name groggily. My voice heavy with sleep from dreams of the past. Pushing off the bed, I glance at the time and notice it's far too early for him to be calling. As I head into the kitchen, I question, "To what do I owe the pleasure of a call from you?"

"Do you remember why you left?" he questions in that rich English accent that's heavier than mine, his voice deeper, and I know he's angry or frustrated.

Even though I've been in America for so many years, I still hold onto mine as if it's the only link I have of my old life. "How could I forget, brother?" I bite out harshly, earning me a dark chuckle from Callan.

"I have news for you, and it's time to get back at the man who stole everything from us." His words have my mind reeling, and I'm suddenly awake. A memory assaults me violently as I shut my eyes, willing it away. But it never leaves.

"Carrick." The voice comes from behind me. I recognize it instantly. The man who raised me to be this monster. Don't get me wrong. I love him, he's my father, but deep down I wish he'd chosen a different life for me. Something other than becoming a man so feared around the country that an utterance of my name sets someone into panic mode.

"Dad." I turn to him, shrugging on the suit jacket for my sister's wedding. I don't want her marrying that asshole, but with the money they can bring to the organization, the marriage is sealed. This life is not something I'd wish on anyone. That's why I plan to leave once the nuptials are over.

I'm flying to America where I can be normal. Or at least try to be.

"I need you to finish a job for me. Tonight." That's not a request; it's an order. My father doesn't ask permission. He also doesn't allow anyone to refuse him. Especially his sons.

"I want to leave once it's done. I'm taking Aurora with me," I tell him, knowing he'll have something to say since he doesn't like my choice in women. However, he can't dispute our relationship since she's the daughter of his business partner. Also, she's the first and only girl who can handle my dark needs.

"I think you're making a mistake, but . . ." His words trail off as he places his hand on my shoulder, offering it a squeeze. "I'm always here for you. Family first and forever." The utterance of our motto is enough to have guilt weighing heavily on me. The tattoo on my back that I got when I turned eighteen burns my skin now as realization hits that I'm about to walk out on the family I'm meant to stand beside.

"First and forever," I respond, nodding as he offers me a smile and leaves me in the dressing room. The music that filters through the open door is my signal, so I make my way out to the back of the church, finding my sweet sister smiling

at me. Her arm through our father's, her long, flowing white gown trails behind her.

The march into the church is planned to the T. When the priest starts his sermon, I lose focus. Something in my peripheral causes me to turn. When I do, I notice the glint of black metal. Instinct has me diving for Cayleigh first. My body cocoons her as the shots are fired.

Bang. Bang. Bang.

I lose count how many thunderous bullets zip past me, and in the maelstrom, I can't see my father. I can't see Aurora. My heart hammers in my chest, threatening to break through. People are panicking. There's chaos everywhere, and I see red splattered around me, on me.

Screaming echoes in the emptying church, but I can't move. Protecting my sister is the only thing I can do. I don't know how long I lie there holding a sobbing woman in my arms, but when the silence hangs heavy around us, I lift my head, turning my gaze to the door now swung wide.

Bodies. Blood. Death.

This is my life. It always will be. I need to leave tonight. No more jobs.

"Are you okay, Leigh?" I turn to my sister whose make-

up is racing down her cheeks in black trails of emotion. She nods, but her lower lip trembles. "I need to see who's hurt. Stay down," I order. Pulling my revolver from my holster, I rise to find a massacre.

"Rick!" A shout comes from my left. My brother and father are there, safe. Caked in blood, but alive. When I meet my father's gaze in question, he shakes his head.

I drag my gaze to the place I didn't want to look, but I force myself to. Aurora is lying in a pool of crimson liquid. Her body lifeless. Her eyes closed forever. I drop to my knees as the anguish settles around me, dragging me into a dark abyss of sadness.

I can't breathe. My hand has a grip on the gun. It's the only thing keeping me grounded. A harsh cry rips from my chest, right from my very fucking soul. An anguished, pained sob as I stare at the woman I love lying dead on the ground.

I pull her into my arms. Her lips are parted slightly as if she was trying to say something. A bloom of hope unfurls itself like a flower when she stirs, her eyes fluttering.

"Tigress," I murmur, hoping this is all just a bad dream.

"I'll love you always."

Her final words fall from her lips, and that's when I know

I've lost the only woman I'll ever love. She falls limp in my arms. I don't cry. My eyes are dry as I take her in, but the ache in my chest is unbearable. Irreparable.

Anger, vengeance, and guilt grips me in that moment.

And I vow on the altar in the church I was baptized in, I'll find my revenge.

Slamming my hand on the counter top, I growl out down the line at my brother, "What the fuck did you call me for?"

"News, Rick. Calm yourself down, fecker," he curses as his accent reminds me I'm no longer where I should be -- with my family. "It's time you finished this, Brother. Moran had a man inside the church before we even arrived that day. We've got him here, but his son is in Chicago. He's on business, unassuming. It's time you got revenge. An eye for an eye, Rick."

When we couldn't find the asshole who killed Aurora, I walked out. I didn't give up, but I couldn't put myself through the agony of knowing I couldn't avenge her murder. That led me to packing my shit and moving here. That's when I found a life in the darkness. I found pleasure in as many women as I could. They all mean absolutely nothing to me because they're not her.

I play.

I fuck.

And I close myself off to everything around me. It was only when I found Eva that I found myself caring. Not in the way she wanted, but we both got what we needed from each other at the time.

I can't love another woman after Aurora.

"I'll make sure the asshole pays. Give me his details."

"Listen to me, Rick, this man is worse than his father ever was. He's young and stupid, but he has an army of guards with him. I—"

"I can handle myself, Callan," I tell him. My voice rising in frustration. I've taken down men worse than that fucker Moran. If my brother thinks I'm not capable, I'll show him I'm more grown up than he ever was. When I left, my brother, who's only a year older than me, took over the family business of making sure men paid for their sins. But I know my father had more underhanded dealings than he let on. And I have a feeling the shooting was revenge for something my father did.

Everyone here in my new life knows me as Carrick Anderson, but none of them know my true name—Carrick Aedan O'Leary. Our family goes back centuries in Chicago, linked to the Irish mobsters, and that's the reason I chose to come here.

With my father's property development organization based in London, that's where I spent my younger years, allowing me to easily hide my accent on jobs. Once someone hears the Belfast accent, they're more likely to be wary because Northern Ireland is known for the dangers that lurk beneath the shiny veneer. And since I've been here, it's easier to hide my ancestry. One reason was to move on, the other was to find my own way without the O'Leary name holding me back.

"I'm just warning you, arsehole."

"I know," I tell him. Watching the thick coffee drip into the cup, I envision making the asshole bleed. Soon I'll be watching his blood drip from my fingers. "I've been waiting for this and have much more at stake than you have, Cal. Just send me the details, and I'll see to it he's dealt with."

A sigh greets me from the other end of the line. "I'll

send it in a few minutes."

"How's Leigh?" I ask, missing my sister as I wonder how things would be if I hadn't walked out. If her fiancé wasn't murdered in cold blood.

"She's . . . I don't know, Rick. She's still struggling." The agony in his voice startles me. "Her job is good, distracting, but it's when she's alone. I hear her crying at night. She still has those fucking nightmares."

"I'm buying her a ticket. She's going to stay with me for a while," I tell him, making up my mind. I wasn't there for her the way I should've been. I need to make this right.

"You sure you want her in your shit? Since you didn't want me there?" His chuckle grates my nerves. My brother knows what sort of kink I enjoy, only because he's the one who walked into the club and told me that he's here for the pretty women. He's an asshole. So am I. But at least I admit it.

"Send her over. I'll take care of her," I tell him, picking up the coffee cup now filled with dark liquid. Taking a sip, I revel in the heat and bitter taste.

"If she gets into—"

"She's a fucking grown woman, Callan. If she wants to do something, I'm not stopping her," I bite out angrily. I know Leigh. She's sweet, beautiful, and this life won't appeal to her. And if it does, I'll cut the fucker's dick off who comes near her.

"Yeah, you say that now . . ." he warns, his words tapering to a silent warning.

Sighing, I question, "Is that all you needed?"

"Aye, see you soon, brother." He hangs up before I have time to respond with a *fuck you too*. We've had our fights growing up, but I know Callan is the only person who will forever have my back.

Dropping my phone on the marble top, I head back into the bedroom. My body tingles with anticipation of finally making the fucker who killed Rory pay. I don't remember a time when revenge didn't flow through my veins, and I can't recall a moment when vengeance wasn't at the forefront of my mind.

The only time I ever had any semblance of normalcy is when I'm fucking. My mind is blank. This is the only reason I've spent the past few years indulging in women. As many as I can because the memory of Aurora burns me every moment of the day. She was the only woman who could disarm me. Her long, flowing, honey-blonde locks reminded me of strung silk. And her eyes, the color of jade, seemed to always pierce the armor I wore so savagely.

Heading into the bathroom, I turn on the double showerheads, and I step under the cold spray. It jolts my system harshly, readying me for the day ahead. Running Sins is part of my life now. Along with Mason, my partner, we have made a living by allowing people a safe place to harness their darkest desires.

Closing my eyes, I allow the now scalding water to cascade down my body. Moran is so close I can taste his blood on my tongue. It's been years coming. After he went underground, we searched high and low. He's evaded us for far too long. A smirk tilts the corner of my mouth at what's to come.

Once Callan sends me the information I need, I can plan and ensure Aurora's death is not in vain. What happens after that, I don't know. Sadness claws at me. The memory of her still fresh in mind as if she's with me right now.

Shaking the feeling off, I close the taps and step out into the chilly room. I glance in the mirror, taking in my naked form. The scars of the past dot every part of my chest, abdomen, and my upper thigh. All from fights I've had before. From an ugly past, which I hope doesn't follow me into the future.

When I glance up, I notice it's almost six in the evening. The day has passed by, and when Callan's email came through at midday, I set in motion my plans to corner Moran. Pushing up from my desk, I stalk toward my office door, pulling it open to find a tiny blonde with her back to me.

I'm guessing she's one of our new barmaids standing there like she's lost. Mason must have hired her. I step out of my office, pulling the door shut behind me.

"What the fuck do you want?" I grunt out harsher than I expected. When she spins around, my breath is knocked from my lungs as jade orbs pin me with a glare so ferocious I feel it like a punch to the gut. As if a ghost is standing before me, all I see is her resemblance to the woman I lost.

She doesn't respond at first, which grates on my nerves. Her small chin juts out in confidence, and her eyes narrow as she regards me.

"I asked you a fucking question." I expect her to cower, but she shocks the shit out of me when she squares her shoulders, meeting my gaze dead on.

"I'm Peyton. Should you really be speaking to Savannah's best friend like that?" she retorts hotly, and I find for the first time in years my dick gets hard for a woman with hair the color of gold and eyes the color of green gemstones.

"Why are you standing at my door?" I ask, ignoring the fact that she's just told me who she is. Savvie is going to have my balls for being rude to her friend, but I don't give a fuck. I eat up the distance between us as I step closer to her, and the scent of orchids hits me right in the nose. When I lean in, her fragrance only intensifies. She lifts her eyes to meet mine. The heat of them burns me right to the fucking core.

"I'm here for Savvie, Carrick," she bites out angrily. Her delicate hands press against my shirt, pushing me hard, causing me to stumble backward. *Fucking bourbon.* "She told me you're an asshole, but I didn't take you for such a dick." Her voice is melodic, and even though she's just insulted me, I can't help but want to hear more.

"You have a fiery little mouth. Rather than standing in my club talking to me like that, I can put it to better use." I smirk when her cheeks bloom with a gentle rosy hue. What she said about Savannah has me pondering why the girls have been talking about me.

Savvie is one of my best friends by default since she's Mason's submissive. But it's her personality that makes everyone around her feel the need to be good. She's always there, just waiting for you to do your best, but in my case, my worst. The beauty that's stolen more than just my partner's attention but his heart, too, is something of an enigma.

With her sensual curves, long, flowing, white-blonde hair, and her striking blue eyes, she's every man's fantasy. But it's more than that. She has an air of authority, even in her submissiveness. She exudes a fierce personality that makes her a handful.

I stalk by the petite woman glaring up at me, but

when I head down the hallway, I hear her shoes click behind me. "Why are you following me?" I question harshly, not wanting to look at her, because my heart can't take it. She's the spitting image of Aurora, right down to her sassy mouth.

"I'm looking for Savannah. Can you please take me to her?" I stop at her question. Turning to face her, I smirk. My mouth curls into one of those signature grins that seem to appease any woman. She said please. That's how I like my women, obeying and respecting me.

"Seems like the feisty little minx can be a tamed kitten?" I quip, facing her completely. She's about a head shorter than me, and I wonder what it would feel like having her body above mine. It's the first time in years a blonde has grabbed my attention like this.

"Don't get your hopes up. I'm only asking because I was taught manners. Something it seems you're lacking." Her response makes me chuckle. Sweet, sexy, and sassy. I love it.

"Clearly you don't know how to respect a Dominant."

"Ah, so that's why you're acting like an asshole.

You know, Carrick, being a Dom doesn't give you the right—"

I break off her tirade by grabbing her face, crashing my mouth on hers, feeling her lips mold to mine. Her lips open on a gasp which I swallow, licking into her sweet mouth, tasting every inch of her delicious flavor. The hint of mint and lemon seems to intoxicate me, making me drunk on just the one harsh kiss.

Finally, I break away from her to find her green eyes glistening with both desire and burning with anger. She rears back, and her hand makes contact with my face in a slap which stings her more than it does me.

"Don't ever kiss me without my permission," she scolds me with anger hanging on every syllable. I watch as she grasps her hand, rubbing the palm in circles. A smile cracks on my face as she glowers at me, possibly wanting me to shy away, but she has no idea who she's dealing with.

"I never ask permission for anything I do, Pet," I tell her, leaning in to brush my lips over her ear. "And let me make one thing clear. The next time you attempt to slap me, I'll spin you around so fast, bend you over anywhere we are, and spank your sweet little ass so hard you won't be able to sit down for weeks. Do you understand me?"

I don't wait for her to answer. Instead, my tongue darts out, trailing along the shell of her ear, causing her to shudder in response. I shouldn't be doing this. She's a distraction. A ghost I have no reason to be kissing. But deep down I wonder if she's here for a reason.

"Good girl," I utter, then turn to walk away. She doesn't follow. She doesn't say anything more, and I saunter into the club with a smile on my face. My chest feels tight with the reminder of the past, but there's also a lightheartedness to the banter. I've missed a woman who gives back, and perhaps my soul feels released, free from the cage for a moment. Confusion settles around me as I head to the bar and order a drink.

Almost eight years, and I've never had such a need to take a submissive back to my room and show her exactly what I'd like to do to her. Savvie didn't tell me her friend was visiting, but now that I know, I can't wait to see more of the little minx.

Dylan sets my drink down, and I offer him a nod. "Thanks," I tell him as I lift the glass and press it to my lips. The club is full already, and it's not even seven yet. I wonder if the little blonde will want to play, because my dick is hard, and I'd love to sink it deep inside her tight body.

Four

Peyton

Insufferable asshole, I think to myself as I make my way down the staircase. When I reach the main area of the club, I notice him rising from his bar stool and stalking toward the back where a long, dark hallway beckons. Although I can't fault him on the kiss, I can't believe he actually did it. My body is still thrumming from the electric currents that shot through me when his lips made contact with mine.

He's taller than I pictured, probably around six-four, with broad shoulders, and lean muscle beneath his tailored suit. His messy hair, the color of syrup, and those eyes. In the dimly lit hallway, they pierced me with their golden intensity, but the playful greens and browns danced in them. He had a day-old stubble on his chin, which causes me to lift my hand to my own, feeling the friction.

The man knows how to make my toes curl, which has me wondering what else he can do. My inexperience in this life, in this sordid world Carrick lives in, is evident as I think about what Savvie's told me. I know Mason. I've known him for a long time, but nothing prepared me for the moment Savannah, my best friend, told me she was into spanking and whipping, and even rope play.

I wonder how dark Carrick's hunger goes. How much of this does he really enjoy? I've heard about sadists, the pain they love to inflict, which makes me wonder how any woman can want that.

All men are the same though. Michael was evil, dangerous, and he took and took from me until he left me with nothing but a shell of who I once was. When I learned the truth about him, it hurt me right down to my core that all those years spent together he lied every moment.

But that is my fault.

I almost gave him everything. What's left is just a broken mess.

"Peyton!" My best friend's voice comes from beside me, and I realize I'd wandered to the hallway where Carrick had disappeared and didn't even realize it. Is my subconscious really that desperate for an asshole like him? "What are you doing back here?"

"I'm not sure. I was looking for you, and—" I cut myself off, because for some reason, I don't want anyone to know what happened between Carrick and me. I don't know why, but deep down I feel like keeping It to myself. "I wanted to see what the lure was," I tell her instead, causing those big eyes to narrow in suspicion.

"Uh uh." Her disbelieving response is expected. "Come on, I'll get you a drink. I wanted you to meet Eva tonight. She was supposed to go out with us, but . . . Well, she's rather tied up at the moment." Savvie smiles as she says this, and I know exactly what she means. This *lifestyle* has always been a mystery to me. Since my best friend told me about it. Yes, I've Googled things she's mentioned and found myself rather intrigued. I expected to be horrified, but there was something alluring about it. Call it curiosity. I just hope this kitty doesn't get killed.

Since I'm still so innocent, I wonder if any of the

men in here would want to take on a virgin. Someone to perhaps train and mold. Maybe it's time to test the waters. Surely one man in here would want to have someone pure. Show me the bite of his flogger, or something like that.

"So . . ." I start as we reach the bar, but my words filter into silence when my eyes land on Carrick, who's back in the club and at one of the booths with a beautiful brunette in his lap. He's talking to another man I don't know, but it's the way his hand is possessively gripping her ass that causes me to falter.

"That's Carrick Anderson; he's Mason's partner. Total gentleman, when you get him on his good side, but if you ever walk into him in a bad mood, it's like a tornado taking down anything in his path," my best friend informs me, whispering conspiratorially in my ear.

"He doesn't look that scary," I tell her, eventually dragging my gaze away from him and meeting Savannah's knowing stare. "What?"

"No. Oh, no, no, no. You are not going near Rick," she tells me, wagging her finger in my face. Even though she's older than me by a year, you'd think there was a bigger age gap the way she admonishes me. "He is not someone for you. At all. Ever." She's adamant, but she knows how stubborn I am.

"Please, what can he do? I mean—" Flitting my eyes to him, I notice his heated stare on me. While keeping direct eye contact with me, he tugs the brunette down, kissing her almost violently. His one hand gripping her ass cheek causing my heart to slam against my chest wildly and my thighs to squeeze together as my core tightens with need. An ache so profound steals my breath, and I want to know what his hands would feel like on my body, on my ass, and even stroking my now wet panties.

He demands my attention, holds my curiosity, and I'll be damned, but he makes me want him.

"He's intolerable. Should he be doing that in the middle of the club?" I ask, meeting Savvie's gaze.

She shrugs it off as the barman sets glasses down in front of us. When she finally takes a peek at her boyfriend's partner, she smirks. "He's a little . . . overbearing."

I think for a moment before voicing my opinion. "That's not the word I'd use," I respond. Lifting the drink to my lips, I take a long sip of the minty cocktail. The alcohol hits my bloodstream, the ice causing the glass to frost over, but nothing can cool me down from the way Carrick has turned me molten.

"And what is the word that you would use?" A deep, smooth voice comes from behind me, causing me to pivot into the solid chest of Carrick Anderson, my drink drenching both of us in sticky, clear liquid.

"Shit!" I lift my gaze, meeting his burning one as he smirks.

"I wanted to get you wet, but that's not what I had in mind." His tone is playful yet commanding, and I can't look away. The man is every bit as handsome under the lights of the club than he was in the darkened hallway where he stole a kiss from me.

"Don't be an asshole," I bite back, but the falter in my voice is enough to tell him I don't mean a word I say. I want him to be that. I want him to take me right here on the bar.

Calm down, Pey. You're like a bitch in heat.

"Okay, you two." Savannah rescues me from the searing torment of Carrick's penetrating gaze. "Let's get you cleaned up." She tugs on my arm, but before we can leave, Mason saunters up to us, taking in the scene before him.

"Hi, Pey," Mason says in his thick accent while he leans in to brush a kiss on my cheek, then turns to Savannah. "I need you, Sav. There's a girl who needs some support in the rope room. She's tensing up too much," he orders. "I'm sure Rick can show Peyton to the change room to get cleaned up."

"I can certainly do that." Carrick's words drip with desire. His hungry gaze never falters as he regards me. "Let's go, Kitten," he says, turning on his heel, walking toward the staircase I'd earlier descended.

"I'll be okay," I tell Savvie before rushing to keep up with the man who I can't seem to keep my eyes off of. The way his slacks hug his thighs, the roundness of his ass taunting me as I take each step behind him. Once we reach the top, he holds out a hand to me, and I allow mine to slip into his. The gesture is slight, a gentlemanly one, but his grip on me is more than friendly. As if he's trying to hold on and not let go.

He doesn't say a word as he shoves open a door to a cloakroom. It's plush, elegant with walls of soft cream. The chandelier shines an intricate pattern against the surfaces. The gleaming drops of glass hanging from the ornate fixture flash with a gentle golden light as we step inside the bathing room. There are cubicles which have doors the color of raven's feathers, and they're all shut. A black pincushion sofa of what looks like smooth velvet sits in the center of the space, and sinks line a wall of mirrors.

"You can wash up. I'll grab something for you to wear," he says. Releasing my hand, he leaves me in the immaculate room. The mirror on the wall reflects my wet T-shirt, showing off the pink bra underneath. *Great. He's probably got an eyeful.* I pull off the wet shirt, dumping it in the basin.

Opening the tap, I grab some paper towel and wipe the sticky alcohol off my skin, leaving me glistening. I don't hear him when he finally returns. Instead, I feel him behind me. His heat cocoons me, causing me to want to melt into it, but I don't.

"This should fit," he whispers in my ear. When I glance at my reflection, I meet his softened yet commanding gaze. His eyes are the color of warm honey, shimmering with longing, which makes me curious as to what he's hiding. Their golden depths hold pain, so much agony it causes my heart to lurch in response. He sets a black shirt on the counter beside the basin without touching me, and I want to sigh in relief and disappointment. But then he lifts his hand, his knuckles brushing along my bare arm in a white-hot trail. Goosebumps dot my skin. A tingle shoots through me.

The air is electric. My nipples harden against the soft lace material of my bra. He drops his eyes to my chest, and I watch as the color darkens to a hazel shade as he takes me in.

"Are you affected by me, Kitten?" His words feather over the sensitive skin of my neck, causing a slight tremble to trail through me. My stomach tightens, swirling with desire, twirling wildly as if a hurricane is about to pull me into the eye of the storm and I have no way of stopping it. I want to retort. I want to answer back with an angry bite, but I can't, because when I open my mouth to form words, I can't find them.

His hand comes up as he tenderly strokes the curve of my nape, moving my hair to the side. It allows him access to the most sensitive part of my neck. Just behind my ear. The movement is so light I'm sure I'm imagining it, but my eyes are glued to his touch in the reflection. The skittering of an electric current shoots down my spine, and I pull my lower lip between my teeth, biting down to keep from moaning out loud.

"Or am I the only one who feels this delicious poison trickling between us?"

Once again, he only breathes the words. They're carried along my flesh like a map leading directly to the apex between my thighs. My fingers grip the material of the shirt he set down, and I finally clear my throat.

I'm about to answer when his finger reaches up, finding my lips and pressing against them to shush me. He places his other hand flat against my stomach, fingers fanned out, his pinky just touching the waistband of my jeans.

"This isn't a good idea, Carrick," I tell him, even though his finger is still positioned on my mouth. His hand inches down. I tremble. I'm needy and wet. With deft fingers, he unbuttons my jeans, slipping his hand beneath the material but keeping it above my panties.

"Tell me no, Kitten," he murmurs in my ear as he strokes me slowly, tentatively. His movements are nothing like I'd expect a domineering asshole to be. "Please tell me to stop," he urges me, implores me with a pained growl.

"I-I . . ." My words are decimated when his finger trails over my clit. He presses down, and I'm beyond reason. My hips buck against his hand. I'm drenched. So fucking turned on I'm ready to bend over and beg him to take me every which way.

"Peyton," he chants my name, as if he's a sinner asking for salvation. Repenting for much more than his ministrations on my body. He's playing me like a musical instrument. As if he's the master, attuned to my moans, knowing what to press to draw out my whimpers. Which button to push to cause me to cry out as an orgasm rocks me to my very core, and he's not even entered me with his cock or his fingers. I turn to putty in his hands. Nothing ever felt like that with Michael. It was a chore for him to kiss me most times, which is why I'm still a virgin.

We stand there in silence for what feels like hours, but when I open my eyes, I don't care how long I've been in his arms, because I want more of what I can't have. He's a bad idea, but I've been known to make stupid decisions. "Carrick, this . . . This . . . It can't—"

"It's already happened, Kitten." He pulls his hand from my jeans. Turning me around, he trails his finger, wet with my juices, over his full pink lips. I watch in awe as he slowly licks at the arousal. "This" — he gestures between us with his index finger— "is happening because you no longer have a choice but to be mine."

"Don't flatter yourself. I'm no submissive, Carrick. I came here to experience it, not to be owned. You can't just lay claim to me because you made me come," I return hotly. Grabbing the shirt he left for me, I shrug it on and storm out of the room, leaving him glaring at my back. Once the door shuts, I lean back, inhaling deeply.

"Are you okay?" Savannah's voice startles me back to the present when I almost walk into her, and I nod, biting my lip to keep the tears at bay. "What did Rick do?"

"Nothing. He didn't do a thing. I need a drink," I tell her in frustration at my stupidity. I'm such a slut for Carrick. One moment I'm telling him no, the next he's stroking me to orgasm. Heading down the stairs to the main area of the club, I reach the counter to find the barman whose name tag reads *Dylan*.

He glances at me, offering me a friendly smile. "What can I get you?"

"Tequila. Make it double," I tell him.

He nods, smirking at Savvie who's standing beside me, waiting for my confession. She knows me too well, and sometimes I feel as if I need space. Just time away from everything and everyone.

"He didn't do anything that I didn't want," I tell her without looking at my best friend. I can't see the *I told you so* look on her face. She doesn't respond. Dylan sets two shots on the counter, and I pick one up, clinking mine with hers, we down the shots in one gulp. If there's one way of getting rid of these emotions, this pain, it's to meet the bottom of a bottle of tequila.

Five

Carrick

For two days, I've been sitting in my office with her on my mind. Work has been put on the back burner. Reading the emails and applications coming through for staff blur in comparison to the light she shone as she peeked up at me. Watching her lose all control was the most intoxicating thing I'd ever seen.

She burned at my touch, and I was scorched by her heat. There is something about her, the smile she hides from me, those glistening jade orbs of emotion that dance with wicked mischievousness. I want her.

With every person I've spoken to over the past forty-eight hours, with each moment I've spent attempting to focus on the business at hand, her sounds echo in my mind. They're still the only thing I can think of. I try to concentrate on the documentation Callan sent over, but the sweet kitten has been running circles in my head.

Her feisty nature drew me to her, but it's the blonde hair and green eyes reminding me of Aurora that has me hooked. Maybe it's wrong to want a girl who looks exactly like the woman I lost, but I can't help it. I'm a selfish asshole, and this time I'm going to ensure I get what I want.

I can't quell the thirst I have for her. Since she walked out, leaving me drenched in her sweet juices, I've been craving another taste. One more.

Can a night with Peyton allow me to say goodbye?

Would it be a bad thing to indulge in her?

All the nights I prayed for Aurora to come back to me, and now her doppelgänger is right here, and I have the opportunity to get the closure I've longed for.

It's been such a long time since I've given a second glance to a blonde, but it was like seeing a ghost. A living, breathing ghost. When she walked out, it took all my fucking restraint not to follow her. I wanted to own her, lay claim to a woman I'd just met. Only because she reminds me of someone. She reminds me of a past I lost.

It's not fair. I shouldn't do it, but I can't stop myself

from wondering if Peyton had said yes, would I have really been able to see her for her? Perhaps it's time I find out. If she's Savvie's friend, she knows exactly what this lifestyle entails. That means she was in here for a reason. That thought causes a smile to crack on my face. It's genuine. The first one for a long while.

No submissive has ever walked away from me before. But no other woman makes me want to bind her to my bed for days while I fuck her senseless. Not like Peyton. Each toy I've played with has been forgettable. Every woman I've touched has never given me a forty-eight hour hard on like the beautiful, intoxicating Peyton.

While I was deep in conversation on an online conference call with a new rope supplier, all I could think of was the way she moaned my name. How her slight curves trembled as she found euphoria from my touch. Since that night, I haven't seen her, nor heard from her. When I asked Savvie for her number, I was politely told to go fuck myself. Savannah is a fiery little toy.

I figured I'd be able to cast her from my mind, but sitting here has only proven one thing. It's time to take a chance.

Both nights I've been down in the club looking for her, but she's not visited again. I don't know where she's staying, not even my best friend, Mason, will tell me. I know why though. Savannah would have his balls if he so much as uttered a word.

Since we each have a penthouse above the club, I know she's not in the building. I would have seen her coming or going, so the only other option would be one of the many hotels close by. I have gone so far as to call a few asking for her, but none of them will divulge information about their guests.

All I have to go on is her name, Peyton Moore. Another blonde Irish girl that's gone and caught my attention and doesn't want to let go.

"My name is Aurora O'Neil," the woman before me says with a fire that sets my body alight. I know exactly who she is. There's no need for her to tell me anything more. The name alone tells me she'll one day be my wife.

"And I'm Aeden O'Leary," I answer, not giving her my first name. Instead, I tell her the name she'll recognize. We've been told from a young age we'll one day be married. Who

knew people still did that? My father and hers are old friends. Business partners in a way.

Going back centuries through our ancestry, an O'Neil and O'Leary have always been married. To keep the business in the two families who had joined together and formed a section of the Irish mob.

"Why do you lie?" she quips, while her green eyes trail over me in a descent of every inch of my body. Her eyes leave sizzling desire in their wake, which causes me to groan deep in my throat.

"What do you mean?"

"Your name is Carrick," she tells me easily, folding her arms in front of her chest. Her tits, those beautiful mounds, lift, and so does my dick.

"Aye, it's Carrick Aeden O'Leary," I respond, trying to keep my voice even but failing as the rasp is easily noted. Her right eyebrow arches in question, then her mouth tilts into a smile. A movement that turns a light on in her face, making her look like an angel.

"Then why didn't you say so, Carrick?" she says, stepping closer to me. "Because," she starts, her finger tracing a line from just below my left eye, down to my lower lip. "I'd

like to kiss you, Carrick." She breathes my name, which makes my dick jolt to attention.

"You wouldn't want to kiss a man like me, princess," I tell her, dropping my mouth closer to hers.

Her head tips to the side. She narrows her gaze, watching me. "And why is that?"

"I have blood on my hands. I'm no good for you." It's true. I kill. I've watched men bleed from wounds I've inflicted, and the worst thing is, I enjoyed it.

"Who said I wanted a good man?"

And that's how we started. Aurora and me. We'd found love in a world where there was none. She was a girl who would forever be the princess of an Irish mobster, and I would always be the man who killed for her father.

My phone buzzing drags me from the memory of how the past seems to slowly be replaying itself. A beauty and her alluring smile, with eyes that look right through me. The only difference is, Peyton doesn't want me. *Why would she?* I could never give her a ring, or a happily ever after. I'm not the knight, I'm the goddamn dragon. When I pick up my mobile, I glance at the name before swiping my finger over the screen.

"Callan," I answer, waiting for the lecture from my brother about not responding to the email he sent about Moran, but I've had something else on my mind. This is the most I've spoken to my brother since leaving. I can never bring myself to call and hear my father's voice if he by chance answered. His disappointment in me for leaving is enough to break me down, turn me into the teenage boy who always did everything to please him.

"I've told Cayleigh she's staying with you. Her flight leaves on Sunday. They'll land at the private hangar. Make sure you pick her up." Straight to the point as always. We've both grown up with a father who was business always. Strict, but fair, we were taught that commanding respect from anyone we come into contact with is the only way to live. And also, the only way to love.

My mind drifts to two nights ago when a specific blonde challenged me beyond reason.

"Are you listening to me?" Callan's voice cuts through my thoughts.

"Yeah," I clear my throat in response to him. Shifting in my chair, I glance at the time, realizing it's almost time for Savvie and Mason's show. That means *she'll* be there. "I have to go. Just drop all the info to me, and I'll make sure she's collected."

"Fuck you, Rick. Are you hanging up on me for pussy?" Callan hits the nail on the head when he questions me, but I'll never tell him about Peyton. The thing about Callan O'Leary, my older brother, is we've always been in competition, and women have been no different.

"Fuck off, Cal. I have to go." I hang up without waiting for his response because I know he'll get me all the information for Leigh's flight. Pushing off my chair, I head to the window looking out over the club. There at the bar leaning against the dark wood is the curvaceous woman who's somehow invaded my mind, causing me to wonder about who she is, why she's here, and just how I'm going to get her into my bed, in my dungeon, and kneeling to please me.

I turn away from staring at her and pour myself a double shot of whiskey. A three-finger shot is enough to have my body buzzing, but still not too much to cloud my mind. No, there's only one thing I need right now, and she's sitting at my bar dressed in a scrap of material that's about to be ripped off her petite frame and lying on my office floor.

Lifting the glass, I gulp the whole shot in one swallow. The harsh liquid burns as it trickles down my throat. "I'm coming for you, Kitten," I utter as I slam the glass on the bar. When I pivot to the door, I notice it opening, and there on the threshold to my office is the woman in question. The one I want to devour and fuck until I've had my fill.

"Do you always talk to yourself?"

"Only when women deny me what I can so clearly see in their eyes. Those big, doe-eyes you're piercing me with, they tell me all I need to know." I stalk toward her, placing my palm flat on the wood of my door, which shuts it behind her.

"You're overconfident," she retorts, squaring her shoulders. Those green eyes flicker as they look through me, answering me with confidence she doesn't feel. She's here because she wants me; I can see it.

"And you, Little Kitten, are a liar," I tell her, leaning in, caging her against the door with my mouth at her ear. "Tell me, did you touch your pussy last night wishing it was me?"

Her silence answers me.

"And did you come for me?" I quip, stepping back, allowing her space.

"Just because you're overbearing and commanding, doesn't mean you have to be an asshole," she bites back, causing me to chuckle.

"That's not why I'm an asshole, sweetheart. I am one of the most thoughtful, caring Dominants you'll ever find. But my assholeness comes from much more than you can ever fathom. Don't judge a book by its cover." I turn, heading back to the desk. I perch myself on the edge. Crossing my arms in front of my chest, I watch her stalk toward me. Her hips sway just a little more than she needs them to, causing my slacks to feel a tad tighter than they should.

"Oh? Well then you should take your own advice. Just because I'm in your club doesn't make me a submissive. And don't ever think you know what I have or haven't been through."

"You're not submissive? Mmm . . ." I answer, watching her as she stops in front of me. My legs spread, and I crook my finger at her. "Come here, Kitten."

"Why do you call me that?" Her lips purse in frustration, and I'm tempted to test out just how beautiful they'd look wrapped around my dick. But with Peyton, I have a feeling patience will pay off more than the domineering way most women enjoy.

"Because you're a feisty little toy, and you look like you can be a handful. Also, I have a feeling while I'm driving my dick inside you, those claws will come out, and that makes me want to test my theory." My words cause her to raise both eyebrows in response. She steps between my legs as easily as a submissive would, just the way I need her to.

Normally with women, I find myself feeling a pang of guilt, of agony, but with Peyton, it's different. No guilt. No heartache, just lust. Desire is a dangerous thing. It can heal you, but it can also tear you down to your very soul and destroy you.

"Lift your dress," I tell her, expecting a retort, but

she surprises me by obeying. I, in turn, raise my eyebrow in question to her responsiveness.

"If you want a sub so badly, then teach me," she says, causing my cock to harden painfully. It's thick, solid, and throbbing to drive deep inside her pert little ass. Between those luscious tits, and inside her pussy that I'm dying to taste.

"You're too new to this life. I can't train inexperienced submissives," I tell her, placing my hands on her hips, tugging her closer. I don't trust myself with this woman. She's dangerous to me, to my heart, because when her gaze meets mine, I feel it. A thump. A thud of emotion. Of need I squashed long ago. Emotion is not one of my strong suits, because when I allowed it to take over me all those years ago, it annihilated me, and I lost everything. I vowed to never allow it inside me again.

"Are you scared of me?" She tips her head to the side, regarding me with a smile dancing on her full, shimmering lips. They're pink, plump, ready to swallow a cock.

"I'm not scared of anything, Kitten." I allow my hands to grip her ass cheeks, squeezing them in my grasp. Her lace underwear feels smooth against her skin. Her little bubble butt is enough to have me coming in my goddamn slacks.

"Then teach me, Carrick," she utters, breathing my name. Her delicate hands land on my shoulders. Her touch does things to me. Things I shouldn't feel, and I should definitely not need.

"Would you be able to handle me?"

"You said you're a thoughtful and caring Dominant." She throws my words back at me, and I'm mentally kicking myself for telling her that. I said it to make her want me, but now that she does, I don't know what to do with this . . . desire.

"I am," I affirm.

"Then . . ." her words tinker into nothing when I trail my hand over the right cheek of her ass, my fingers finding her apex. My middle finger strokes her slit. The heat emanating from her is addicting. I stroke her pussy lips, feeling the smoothness below the lace. *Fuck.* She's bare.

"Is your pussy smooth?" I ask. She nods. "Have you ever been eaten out?" My question causes her to blush, but she nods again. "Not by me," I tell her, my finger now pushing the lace into her hole, drenching it in her sweet arousal. Her scent filters up to me, and I can't help inhaling her. *Jesus Fucking Christ.* I lift her. Turning around, I place her on the desk, shoving her thighs apart.

"Carrick."

"Shh," I grunt, dropping to my knees. I grip the scrap of black material hiding what I need and rip it from her body in one harsh tug. "Good God, Kitten, you have a beautiful little cunt," I growl. Leaning in, I don't wait for her to respond and lap at her smooth lips.

"Oh God!" Her cry is loud as I suck her clit into my mouth. My teeth graze the hardened nub of flesh, pulling and tugging at it as her hands find purchase in my dark hair. She tugs and pulls at me, but I'm in control. Or at least, my version of control. My tongue darts into her hole. It's tight, dripping with slick arousal I drink up like she's my only sustenance.

My fingers press into the sensitive skin of her thighs, and I know I'm bruising her, but I don't stop. My mouth is working her cunt, and I revel in how her back arches into a perfect curve, lifting up from my desk. Her whimpers and mewls grow into an erotic symphony echoing around us, filling my ears with the most beautiful song I've ever heard.

Peyton is lost in her pleasure, and I'm the conductor. She sings, and I tell her what to say. Our movements sync, our pleasure hits its peak as she gushes, her body pulsing around my tongue as slick, musky, sweet honey drips from her into my mouth, feeding me every ounce of the sweetest juices I've ever tasted.

I slow my movements as her body shudders, trembles, and shakes. Her legs are tight around my head, but as she falls limp onto my desk, I release her, rising to watch her eyes flutter open in euphoric bliss.

"Have you ever been eaten out?" I ask again.

She nods. Then, she graces me with a smile that drips beautiful poison onto my dead, blackened heart. That same organ that once loved, ceased to beat for almost eight years. Fear grips me along with need. I want her, but how can I ever be with someone when my heart is not mine to give?

Six

Peyton

When my eyes finally open, I stare at the most beautiful golden eyes I've ever seen. They're sparkling in the dim light with desire and lust. He smiles then, almost ruefully, and I wonder if he's sorry he just made me come all over his desk.

"You're beautiful when you lose control," he rasps with satisfaction. His fingers thread through mine as he murmurs the words. I sit up as he helps me onto wobbly legs.

"I don't often allow myself to feel, to let go." My honesty is raw as my throat burns with emotion. I walked in here to give in to the need I've been feeling for the past two days. Every night when I went to bed, he haunted my mind. Each morning when I woke up, it was his eyes I wanted to look into. It's strange having someone you don't know occupy every part of your day.

He did that to me. And now that his lips glisten with my arousal, I find myself wanting more. More of him. More of this feeling that I am a woman who can be desired.

"Were you serious?" he asks, dragging me from my thoughts, causing my eyes to snap up to his, meeting his curious stare. "You want me to train you? To take you on as a submissive?"

"Yes," I respond. Stepping closer to him, I trail a fingernail down his tie, then I grip it, pulling him closer to me. "I want this," I whisper on his lips. My tongue darts out tentatively to lick the juice from his full lips. The familiar flavor of my desire bursts on my taste buds.

I may be a virgin, but I've played with myself and tasted my own juices from my fingers many times. I was always curious as to why men enjoyed going down on a woman. Michael was more experienced than I was, and when I asked him, he told me every girl is different.

After spending three long years with him, I never trusted him enough to have sex. To give him that part of me. I'm not religious, so I wasn't saving myself for marriage. All I wanted was someone who'd give me the same pleasure I give him.

"If I train you, we do it no strings attached. I don't do well with being tied down," he utters, and I can't stifle the giggle bubbling in my throat.

"Is that why you enjoy tying others down?" It's a playful response to his rather serious words. It earns me a dark chuckle which vibrates in his chest.

"Kitten, if you only knew the things I want to do to you and your perfect little body," he rumbles, his hands finding purchase on my hips as he tugs me closer, pressing what I can feel is a rigid erection against my stomach.

"I can tell, Mr. Anderson," I say, pursing my lips as I press a kiss to his. It's slow, sensual, but as soon as his tongue asks for entry, I allow it easily. He licks into my mouth, tasting me as I do him. It's addictive. This feeling of need that drives people to fuck.

No emotion. No love. Just pure animalistic fucking.

I never understood it. How you can allow someone into your body without feeling anything for them. But the way Carrick kisses me, I can believe that many women have given themselves to him freely. Begged him. Because as scared as I am, I want it.

"There's something I need to tell you first," I whisper against his mouth, sucking his tongue into mine, harder, flicking my own tongue over his. Teasing him. Needing him to make me feel something other than this numbness I've been living with for so long.

"Honesty always. Tell me, Peyton," he says. The darkness that swirls in his eyes remind me that he's a stranger. I may not know everything about him, but I find myself confessing.

"I'm . . . I've never been with anyone." My cheeks heat with embarrassment. I don't know why, but shyness overcomes me in that moment.

"You're a virgin?" His question is pure shock. I lift my gaze to his, meeting his impossibly beautiful golden eyes. I nod. "Jesus." The word is grunted, his fingers press harder into my flesh. "How can you want this life?"

"I want to learn. I want to find ultimate pleasure, but I want you to do it. Savannah's told me a lot about the different things . . . I mean . . . There's just so much . . . Please, Carrick?" I plead. I've heard her stories where she's confessed to feeling free. Of finding pleasure in spanking or being blindfolded and flogged. She's even told me about pinwheels. Small metal spikes used during sensation play. Yes, I'm a virgin, but I've heard enough to know this is what I want.

"If I do, this is between us. We fuck, we play. I'll drop you into the darkest abyss of desire where you'll question yourself, your body, your needs, but you'll want it. Ache for it even. We'll indulge in anything you want to learn." His words only add fuel to the already burning fire within me. "You will learn this life each time we're together. I'm going to push all those rigid fucking boundaries you've become accustomed to. I'm going to break them down. As I take pleasure from your body, you'll find euphoric release each time, that I assure you."

I nod, opening my mouth, but he places a finger on my lips to silence me.

"But one thing I need to make clear, Peyton. You'll give me your body, your mind, but never, and I mean never allow your heart to get involved. It's not what I want. And it's not something I can give back. I only take what I can give in return. This isn't a relationship. It's an agreement."

"No hearts. Got it," I mumble against his finger, which now trails over my upper lip, then my lower one. I open, taking the digit into my mouth while meeting his stare, sucking on it, causing his gaze to darken with unadulterated lust. It's clear, staring back at me, his beast that hides in plain sight comes forth.

"I'm bad for you in so many ways," he remarks with pain hidden behind each syllable. As much of an asshole he was the night I first met him, there's agony lacing his tone. I see the broken man before me, and all I want to do is fix him. But I learned from a young age, you can't change someone if they don't want to be.

I've had *good men* forced upon me by my father before he found Michael. Men he thought would make perfect husbands for his princess. But they were all not interested in the innocence. They wanted girls who they could parade around on their arm. I was the nerdy girl in jeans and Chucks.

"I never asked for a good man," I tell him honestly.

"You should be careful, Kitten. There are men out there who will only use you if you say something like that." He says this to scare me. To give me an out, but I don't take it. Instead, I bite down on his finger, flicking my tongue over the tip, eliciting another deep groan from him.

When I finally release him, I respond, "Like I said before, Carrick Anderson, never judge a book by its cover, because there are always pages that hold the darkest secrets." I want to tell him about my life. About how I grew up and all the things I've seen. I want to give honesty a chance, but like he said, this isn't a relationship.

"Then indulge in my world for a few weeks. Give yourself time to learn, to experiment, and to experience. If it's something you hate, you'll know. If you take to it, then you'll be able to find a Dominant and know what he'll expect of you."

Nodding, I take a step back and toe off my shoes. He watches me like a hunter would watch its prey. That's what he is. A predator.

Before he has time to ask what I'm doing, I drop to my knees before him, my fingers work the zipper of his slacks, and I shove them along with his boxers down. His cock, thick and hard, juts out in my face. It leaks with his arousal, and I lap at it, taking in my first taste of the man who's going to be my owner for a month. Veins trail maps along the rigid shaft, and I lick each one, reveling in his flavor.

"Peyton," he hisses when I take the crown into my mouth, allowing my tongue to dart over the tip, taunting him. My eyes snap up to his, meeting his gaze as he fists my hair. "Jesus," he utters again as I slide his shaft deeper into my mouth.

The movement causes his hips to jerk forward. The head of his cock slips into my throat, causing me to gag. My eyes tear up, but I don't blink. I allow myself to breathe through my nose.

"How does a fucking virgin know how to suck a cock like a slut?" he bites out, pure unadulterated pleasure on his face. He's handsome. He's stunning, breathtaking. I can't believe I'm doing this. "Can you take me all?" He grunts through his clenched teeth, and I know he's barely holding onto his restraint. I don't move my head, but I shift my hands behind my back, giving him wordless consent to take me.

His nod is all I need to know he's about to use me.

With his hands fisted in my blonde locks, he pulls out and drives back into my mouth. The movement causes me to choke again, but he doesn't relent. He takes his pleasure from my mouth.

Again and again.

In and out.

Deeper and faster.

My clit throbs with need to be touched, but I know better. I've read all the books. I recall how Savannah told me stories about not listening to Mason. If he hasn't given me permission, I will not touch myself. He fucks my mouth like a man possessed, and I'm kneeling at his feet, praying for more. My inner masochist awakens, and I want him to hurt me, to give me pained pleasure so profuse I can no longer live without it.

I want everything this man is giving. His body shudders as his cock jerks in my mouth, shooting jet after jet of hot release onto my tongue, and my throat works to swallow quickly. His head drops back then, and he chants my name. He sings it to God above, but I know there's no one up there. I've known that all my life.

In the heart-numbing pleasure that's racing through

my veins, I know the only one who can hear Carrick now is the devil who taunts me from the fires of hell. The one who's gifted me the life I've lived. As much as I want Carrick to believe I'm a sweet, innocent girl, I know deep down my heart is as black as coal. I learned life is one fuck-up after another. So here I am. I fled to Chicago, and I've found someone who can give me purpose.

He slips from my mouth. I lick my lips at the salty taste of his release. Gently, he reaches down, offering me his hand. "There's something about you, Kitten," he says with the lightest touch to my face. Stroking my cheek, he leans in and plants a kiss on my lips. "Something so damn dangerous," he says, not knowing just how true his words are.

"I could say the same about you," I tell him. My eyes rove over him as he tucks himself back into his slacks. Once he's zipped up, he smiles, his gaze on me.

"You've proven to be a good girl so far. We'll test your limits as we go. I want you to sign an NDA, an agreement that we are doing this together. That you're asking me to be your Dominant. It's nothing serious. It's just to ensure we both get what we want out of this."

I turn as he passes me, heading to his chair. He slips into the seat, opens his laptop, and pulls up a document which starts printing behind him.

"And what is it you want out of this?" I question, unsure if I want an answer or not.

He doesn't look at me for a moment, and I wonder if he's going to afford me a response. When he finally drags his attention to me, he meets my questioning gazes and smiles. His mouth curls into a smirk so full of promise, dark and alluring, yet frightening at the same time, It makes me wonder if the stories I've heard about him are true.

"I get you. I get closure. And I get my final goodbye," he tells me confidently, causing me to furrow my brow in confusion. His full lips purse into a tight line.

A serious expression darkens his face, and I know that if I pushed, he'd either punish me, or he'll close off. Even so, I take a chance. "That sounds forbidding. Are you planning on killing me once we're done?" I joke, seating myself on the edge of his desk.

"I'm planning on taking back a part of me I lost a long time ago. Something I will not tell you, but let's just say, as I help you learn, you help me heal."

"A broken man." I nod, watching his eyes darken as he narrows them at me. "What did she do to you?" I ask, knowing I'm pushing buttons because his mouth turns severe. He rises from his chair, rounds his desk, and plants a hand on either side of the wood where I'm sitting. As he leans in, fear skitters down my spine. His expression is thunderous. Almost murderous.

"If you ever ask me something like that again, I won't go easy on you. I'll make those pretty green eyes drip tears all over my hard cock while I shove it in your throat. Then, once you've gagged on my dick, I'll bend you over, whip you until your ass is a bloody mess, and fuck your tight little virgin hole until you're screaming, begging me to stop. However, like I said, I'm not a nice man, so I won't stop. I'll continue owning your body until you're a whimpering mess on the floor. Do you understand me?"

Placing my hands on his chest, I push him away, hop off his desk, and stride over to the bar. Grabbing the bottle he was drinking from earlier, I pour myself a steep shot and down it in one long gulp, savoring the burn.

When I turn to him again, I smile. "I understand," I start, swaying my hips as I near him again. "Let me tell you something, Mr. Anderson. You don't scare me. I may be a virgin, but I've seen worse, been through worse, and I've survived worse. Which means any threat you throw my way, I'll take, I'll own, and I'll walk out on the other side with my head held high and my tight little pussy ready for more."

We stare at each other for a long while. We wage war between each other in those moments. Him needing me, me aching for him. Both dangerous to the other, but not wavering nor walking away. This man may be the one to finally make me fall. And that is the only thing that scares me.

He reaches up. Cupping my face in his hands, he brings his mouth crashing down on mine in a kiss so heated, filled with so much yearning I'm tempted to jump on him and beg him to fuck me right now. My hands grip his shirt, pulling him closer, as if we can climb into each other, to mold ourselves into one form and sear our souls in the darkness it seems we both revel in yet try to run from.

My body yields to his in a way I'd never experienced. His fits along mine like it was always meant to be there. He pulls away, his face a picture of perfection. Angular jaw, prominent full lips, his eyes, those golden-colored orbs, pin me to the spot. His hair is a mess of dark waves, one falling just over his forehead making him look younger. His face almost more youthful than his possible mid-thirties.

"You're quite the challenge, Kitten," he says with pride.

"I'm much more than that, Carrick. So much more." It's not me being overconfident. It's the truth. When I walked away from my life in New York, nothing could stop me from starting fresh. When Savvie told me to come here, to spend time in Chicago with her, I didn't think I'd be walking into an agreement like this.

"Tell me."

Shaking my head at his command, I step away from him, needing space. The claustrophobia seems to strike me then, knowing I'll never be able to tell him who I really am. What I've really done.

"I don't like asking twice, Kitten."

"I thought you said no personal details?" I respond, turning to glance at him over my shoulder. He doesn't answer, merely shrugs. "Don't ask me to give you something you cannot give in return."

"Touché."

With that, I turn, grab the contract which lies on his desk, and leave him in his office. But before I go, I tell him while staring at the wooden door before me. "I'll get back to you with this." I wave the pages and step out into the hallway.

He doesn't follow.

I don't expect him to.

The ball is in my court.

SEVEN

CARRICK

Yesterday has been on replay in my mind since Peyton walked out of my office. Our last and final kiss was the only thing left between us. She took the NDA and went on her way, leaving me wanting to follow. I have no idea what I'm doing. She makes me feel like a goddamn teenager who doesn't know how to handle a woman. It's ridiculous.

Her fire is intoxicating. I want her to burn me. To make me feel something other than the numbness that's enveloped my life. From the outside, I come across as a domineering asshole, and that's partly true, but deep down, at my core, I'm exactly what she called me—broken. Peyton sees me. Everything I hide, she seems to dredge up, and it makes me both angry and feral.

When my door flies open suddenly, I am met with

Mason's hard glare.

"What the fuck are you doing?" he grits out through clenched teeth. His jaw ticks in frustration as he regards me. The man is my height, almost six-five with broad shoulders encased in a blue button-up. His tanned Italian skin looks as if he's been on vacation for months. He has a full head of black hair and stubble that looks like he hasn't shaved this morning. His angry green glare tells me he knows something happened with Peyton.

Slamming the door behind him, he stalks to my desk. I've known him since I arrived in Chicago, and I'd trust him with my life. I know more about him than he even realizes. I always make sure to do background checks on everyone I plan to go into business with, and Mason's had a rough life, but he got himself back on the straight and narrow, and now he's one of the most successful men in the city.

"I don't know what you're talking about." I lean back, my elbows on the arms of my chair, steepling my fingers under my chin as I regard him.

"Cut the shit, Rick. You're going to train a submissive? And not just anyone, you're offering to train Peyton?" I should've known the girls would have spoken about it. Perhaps Peyton needed to talk about what I'm offering her. She should have come to me. We'll have to work on her trust issues. And her damn obedience.

"Yes, I am going to train Peyton," I tell him with a nod.

"No. You're going to tell her you made a mistake, and you're no longer interested. Okay?"

I chuckle at his insistence. I'm not sure what the problem is. I've trained women before. Perhaps it's because she's so new to this lifestyle. This intricately woven web of darkness and desire that mingles like bourbon over ice. As I told Peyton, I'm not the trainer. Granted, I know how to do it. I've just never chosen to.

"This is none of your concern, Mason. My life. My rules. My woman." I don't know where the last two words fit into it, but for some reason, I feel the need to lay claim to Peyton. I told her this was no strings. I made it clear there would be no emotions, but with him forbidding me to take her as a sub, to train her, my feelings seem to skyrocket. He may be my friend, but the asshole will not tell me what I can or can't do.

"She's not yours. This girl has been through too much, Carrick. Normally, I don't care what you do, but she's like a little sister to me. And she's not your type." His words sting, but the memory of how she tastes has been getting me through the hours that have passed since last night.

"You don't know my type," I bite back, anger lacing every word. It's not his fault for saying that. If I were him, I'd be telling myself the exact same thing. He thinks I have a type—brunette, curvy, with soulful brown eyes. What he doesn't know is that the only woman who holds my heart was blonde, petite, and she had the most intense green eyes I'd ever seen.

The other thing he doesn't know is, she's dead. She was murdered in cold blood, and it's my fault.

"I know that she's too sassy for you. She's got fire, and you love your women to roll over and heel for you. Peyton will never do that."

Pushing up, I stalk toward him, getting in his face. It's the first time we've ever had a standoff like this. A fight. But I'm not letting anyone forbid me to do anything again. "You'd be surprised by what she can do. Now, if you don't have anything better to do than to come in here and piss me off, I'd like for you to leave." With that, I turn and head back to my chair, flopping into it with a sigh.

"Fine. Do what you want, but do not, and I mean it, Rick, do not fucking break her heart." He doesn't wait for my response. He turns to leave, and I find myself alone inside my head.

"Aurora," I call out to nothing. Silence greets me as I make my way into the apartment we'd been renting for the last six months. I know she said she was running late at work, but it's hit ten already. "Tigress?" I call to her, stalking down the hallway toward the bedroom.

As soon as the door opens, my eyes are glued to the bed. There in red lace underwear is the woman who will wear my ring. She's beautiful. Her long, blonde hair cascades over the pillows, her lips are plump, shimmering, and I lick my own wanting to taste her. Long, lithe legs casually settle on the dark blue bed sheets that set off her pale skin.

"Hello, Tiger." She giggles as I drop my gun on the dresser where it will sit till morning. Pulling off my tie, I undo

the silver cufflinks and set them down beside my holster and weapon.

Slowly, I unbutton my shirt as I regard her once more. "Did you want me to spank your pretty ass?" She nods, putting on the innocent expression I love on her. When she pushes up, I notice the way her bra shifts, causing her nipples to harden under the soft material.

"Where were you today?" she asks as I pull off my shirt, dropping it on the foot of the bed. Her gaze drops to the bandage covering my ribs. There's no need to tell her because she already knows. A job her father sent me on was a bust. We had to get out of there quickly, but not before the asshole got a knife to my chest.

"Out. You know I can't go into details, Tigress," I tell her, crawling up the bed between her legs where I know I belong. A wince on my face tells her I'm still in pain, but there's no way I'm not fucking her tonight. She can ride me. I love watching her above me, taking her pleasure. This is where I'm meant to be. It's the only place I feel real, like a good man. One who doesn't go out killing people.

"Well, come here. I'll make you feel better," she purrs as I kiss my way up her inner thighs. The smooth skin tantalizing

as I suck and nibble on her flesh.

"Eating your sweet pussy will make me feel better," I growl against the material covering her smooth lips. Her eyes meet mine in a lust-filled stare, and I can't help the ravenous feeling that overcomes me. I need her. I'll always want her. I love her.

I find myself smiling at the memory. The moment I knew she was my forever. That night I fell asleep inside her and woke up to her mouth around my cock. I don't know what I'm doing with Peyton. Knowing how much she reminds me of Aurora is frightening, but it's also her fire that pulls me in.

She's not scared of me. That is clear in her words and how she challenges me. I've never felt so unsure about something, about someone. My phone buzzes, and before I grab it, I already know who it is. When I swipe my finger over the screen, her name is there, waiting for me.

It's her answer.

I know it is.

My thumb hovers over the message app, not

wanting to read her response. If I'm being completely honest, I don't want her to refuse me. I want her. I want time with her, because for the first time since I broke, I suddenly feel an emotion that was lost to me—hope.

Swallowing my anxiety, I tap the screen, and I exhale a sigh at the word glaring at me.

Kitten: Yes

I tap out my response and hit send.

Me: Good girl. Tomorrow, midday, my office.

Time to go home. It's been a long night, and I need to get some shut-eye. My sister arrives soon, I've got all the intel I need on Moran, and I need to make sure when I do pay a visit to the fucker, I'm ready.

I told Callan I'd sort it out, and I'm not one to break a promise. However, I have a feeling when my sister's flight lands in a few days, my brother will be right there with her.

The wrath I know will course through my veins at

seeing that asshole, Moran, will get me through what I need to do. It's been a long road, but the image of Aurora's blonde hair matted in crimson along with her porcelain skin, the pale blue dress she wore ripped and torn, soaked in blood is my fuel. It pushes me to do what I need to. One final kill. Then it's goodbye to my past.

Night time used to be the worst. It was in the darkness that I would imagine her walking into the bedroom, looking me in the eye and telling me she's not dead. That what I saw was a mistake. Those images play in my head, gripping me in both fear and elation. The thought of living a life without her when she's alive and breathing slices through my heart and leaves me gasping for breath. Which is why I have a submissive in my bed each night. Not for the comfort of holding someone but finding a sleeping body beside me reminds me that I'm alone.

When you love someone so wholly and they're ripped away, the cold, empty side of the bed haunts you. I've come to terms with the fact that I'm single, but it's when I reach for someone and they're not there, panic sets in.

When I wake to a stranger, I recall Aurora's funeral, watching the coffin sliding into the furnace and walking away with a box of ash. Handing it to her parents the day after, I said goodbye and boarded a flight to America. I walked away from her, our memories, and I came here to lose myself in every woman I could find. To forget the pain. To hide the agony.

Closing my eyes, I lift my arm, draping it over my face so I can't look at the red taunting numbers telling me it's two in the morning. I don't watch time as it clicks by. Each moment, every minute is another one reminding me I've wasted too much time not finding the vengeance to move on.

Revenge.

There was talk about Moran's men living in Chicago, but they've been elusive for years. Hidden in the shadows. But when Callan told me I was right, and he is here, my fingertips tingle with the need to close the door to my past.

One more life to take. I've killed before; it's not

difficult. It becomes second nature when you've done it enough times.

Aurora's memory is the only thing that will ensure I do make Moran pay for her death. She was my angel. A light in my darkest nights. With both our families deep in the vile depths of mayhem and murder, we'd always found solace in each other. She was trained, skilled with a gun, knife, and even a bomb. Nobody messed with her, not even me. As much as we loved each other, we knew that someday, one of us would no longer be there. No matter how long you train, how many times you pull the trigger, life is precarious.

Organized crime is a life of solitude, and I grew to understand that. And I accepted I'd forever be alone. Until my father and Aurora's came to an agreement. To ensure their livelihood would remain intact, they wanted us to marry. As soon as my father told me about her when I turned twenty-one, I refused to do it. My life had been a party because I acknowledged my fate. With the money I had, my bachelor status was my ticket to endless pussy, booze, and whatever else would blur the horrific images of dead bodies that plagued my mind.

But I realized that person I had become was forever changed the moment she came along.

When I admitted to wanting her, to agreeing to marry her, my family was shocked. They had even gotten so far as to ask Callan to take her as his wife. Which, of course, the asshole refused. He's single, and I doubt he'll ever find a woman who would put up with him.

Also, his playboy lifestyle means far too much to him to give up, and that brings my thoughts back to Peyton. To my new submissive. No. She's not mine, she's mine for now. My phone vibrates on the nightstand, causing me to jolt upright.

Her name flashes at me in the dark, and I don't think twice about answering.

"Are you okay?" Those are the first words out of my mouth as I swing my legs over the edge of the bed. Panic flaring like a wildfire through my body. I'm awake in an instant when she doesn't respond fast enough.

"I'm fine . . . I just . . ." Her words hang in the air, heavy, filled with . . . longing? Furrowing my brow in confusion, I relax, waiting for her to speak. "I've been awake all night, thinking about this thing between us."

"And what were you thinking?"

"I'm nervous," she admits, her voice low, husky, and I can tell she's tired just from those few words. She must be exhausted. I know I am.

"It's normal to be nervous. This life isn't for everyone. I guess you could say it takes a lot of getting used to as well. I'll take it slow. We can take each day as it comes, Peyton. If there's anything you're not comfortable with, you'll call your safe word."

She sighs through the line, causing my dick to harden in my boxers.

"Don't do that," I grunt, raking my fingers through my unruly brown hair.

"What?" I can picture her face scrunched in confusion. It's cute. She's cute. Too fucking beautiful for her own good. Her small button nose, those deep green eyes, and full pink lips that shine when her tongue darts over them.

"Don't breathe down the line like that," I warn her, my voice dropping into a feral growl.

"Why? Does it turn you on?" Her giggle is the next sound that has me groaning. Jesus, this woman is going to be the death of me.

"Yes. Stop."

"What if I told you I was turned on by your voice? You sound angry, but sexy. It's like you're growling at me. Like an animal," she says, her words lowering into a sweet yet sexy whisper in the earpiece, and I'm finding it difficult to ignore the fact that my boxers are now tenting.

"Kitten, I am an animal. I'm feral, dangerous, and deadly. Do you still want to play this game?" I rasp down the line. Hearing her soft gasp tugs on the restraint that I'm clutching onto. How she does this to me, I don't know. I'm the one in charge of the toys I play with, but Peyton has a way of toying with me. Topping me from the bottom. She easily distracts me from what I want, what I need. Control.

"Then punish me." Three little words, and I'm off the bed and tugging on my jeans.

"Where are you staying?" I ask, my tone rabid with hunger. My body is trembling with desire to take her, bend her over and whip her with my belt until her smooth, creamy skin is filled with red welts.

"Why?" Her question is murmured, curiosity filling it.

"Because I'm on my way to you now. And if you don't tell me where you are, when I find you, it will be worse on that little ass."

"I'm renting an apartment on the seventh floor of the Silver Leaf Apartment Building. Number seven-five-nine," she whispers on a gentle moan which only sets me in motion faster than before.

Pulling on my trainers, I grip my thick black leather belt and feed it through the belt loops of my jeans. My white dress shirt I took off earlier is still on the floor. Once I have it in hand, I shrug it on.

"Good girl." I hang up before she has time to respond, and I'm out the door and heading to my car without thinking. I don't know what this girl is doing to me, but I want to find out how she feels around my cock, and I'm going to do it right fucking now.

I put the car in drive and head down the empty street, only passing a few cars on my way. The early morning is chilly, and I can't help wondering how warm she's going to feel. Soft and smooth. Her silky skin will be beneath me soon enough.

When I pull up to the building moments later, a valet makes his way out of the office and directly to me. I round the front of the car and give him a nod.

"Good morning, sir." He offers a sleepy smile.

Chucking my keys in his direction, I tell him, "Look after her." It's all I can muster before making my way to the elevator, not bothering with acknowledging the sleepy security who's sitting in his small hidey hole office. I know where I'm going.

The long ride up to the seventh floor is slow. Anxiety churns in my gut. I want her. Too much. This isn't good. The warnings are ringing in my mind, but I can't stop now. I've already gone too far.

This time, even though I should walk away before we get attached, I can't. I'm already feeling far too much. It's too soon, but hearing her moan, gasp, and whisper on the line snapped all the control and restraint I normally possess.

When the metal doors slide open and spit me out onto the plush midnight blue carpet, I turn left and count the numbers on each door. When I reach the one I want, I lift a hand and offer three knocks. Sharp, abrupt, and commanding.

The door flies open and there, waiting for me in a pair of small pink panties and a white tank top that hugs every curve of her frame is the blonde, green-eyed kitten I'm about to devour.

"Carrick." She utters my name on a moan which turns my blood molten. Lava races through my veins, heating every inch of my body. I'm hungry. I tamper down my savage, but I know soon enough, I'll be taking her. Fucking her. I ache. And she's the only thing that's going to satiate my craving. I want to indulge in her, consume her. I'm a goddamn glutton, and this woman is going to be my end.

EIGHT

PEYTON

He doesn't say anything, merely drinks in my form with his golden eyes. As they roam my body inch by torturous inch, my skin prickles under his gaze. As if a match has been struck, I'm burning from the inside out. When he's had his fill, he snaps those golden orbs back to my face then saunters forward, gripping my hips and tugging me against him.

Slowly, he drops his head. His full lips close to mine, so close I ache for him to kiss me. To devour me, but he doesn't. Not yet.

"You're a naughty kitten, Peyton. Do you know what I do to naughty kittens?" he breathes huskily. His warm, minty breath mixed with whiskey fans over me. It's his own scent. Spicy, intoxicating, and addictive.

"You spank them?" I ask, allowing myself to mold

to him. I'm fucking needy for a man who's about to hurt me. I'm being stupid. I shouldn't allow him to take me. There is no way this is going to end well, but I don't have a choice. I'm already in too deep, riding too close to the line of desire and emotion. I want him. My body, my mind -- it's filled with him.

"I do. And when I'm done, you'll be begging me to fuck you hard. To break that sweet innocence you've held onto for so long. Do you want me to fuck your tight little cunt?" he smirks. Leaning in, he allows his lips to whisper over my skin. The movement sending shockwaves of pleasure racing through me. Each second he's near me, I feel myself letting go. I'm allowing my walls to crumble, and I know it's going to hurt in the end. He will be my downfall. And somehow, I don't know if I can even allow myself to care.

I agreed to it, and this is just the beginning. I don't know who I remind him of. I know he's using me, perhaps to get over *her*, but he doesn't realize just how much I'm using him too. This ache I've had for far too long needs to go away. I want a man to desire me. To feel every bit out of control as I do, and Carrick Anderson is doing that right this minute.

I want to drown in him for as long as I can without allowing my heart to fight its way through my high walls, then I'll walk away.

I tell myself that as he kicks the door closed and walks me into the living room. No other words are spoken. He positions me over the desk, which overlooks the city. It's beautiful, with the stars shining down on the room and the silver moon streaming light in.

I'm bent at the waist. I can't see him, but I feel him. His hand trails white-hot desire through me as he strokes my back. His fingertip on my spine, following the path leading down to my panty-clad ass.

"You're exquisite." His words cause me to whimper. Then the buckle of his belt clinks. "Have you ever been spanked, Kitten?"

I don't answer for a moment, then the harsh swat of his hand comes down on my left ass cheek. It stings, causing me to lift up onto my toes. My fingers grip the edge of the desk as I bite down on my lower lip.

"I asked you a question."

"No, Carrick." My answer is a taunted whisper. I

want to beg for another spank, but I don't. I need to hold on to some self-restraint.

"I'm going to spank you. I'm going to see how much that pretty little ass can take. What is your safe word, baby?" he asks, leaning in, pressing his lips to my cheek.

"Indulge." I feel his smile on my skin.

"Good girl," he murmurs, which sends a rush of pleasure through me. How two simple words can make me feel good, I will never understand. He rises and steps behind me, then nothing. I can't hear anything.

Silence hangs in the air, heavy and foreboding. I wanted this. I asked for it. My body trembles. My arousal pools between my legs, and I attempt to squeeze my thighs together to ease the ache low in my groin.

I'm not sure what he's doing. The quiet is deafening. Anticipation. I've read how Dominants use this tactic to instill patience in a submissive. How the longer we wait, the more aware we are. And I didn't believe it until now. Right here, in this moment, I realize something I've never wanted to admit. I am everything Savvie always said I was. She saw it the moment we met. I'm a sub, and there's no turning back.

My mind is so focused on my realization I don't realize Carrick's moved. I'm about to question him when his hand cracks down loudly on my left ass cheek. The sting tingles over my skin, causing the flesh to heat.

He hasn't taken my panties off yet. He rains down another three slaps on either cheek, making me yelp each time. Each one harder than the last. My whimpers turn to moans. My clit throbs, my pussy soaking through the material of my underwear.

"Carrick, please." A whimper falls from my lips, and he halts his assault on my ass. I can hear his breathing at my ear.

"Tell me," he utters on the shell of my ear. The warmth of his breath, of his body cocoons me, sending an excited trickle down my spine. "I want the words from those beautiful lips. I need to know what you need from me so I can deliver it," he informs me.

"I want more."

"Do you want my belt, Kitten?" he purrs in my ear, and I nod. I hear the movement of his hands on the leather, the clink of the buckle as he readies it.

Then the swat on the right globe of my ass causes me

to cry out. But even as the sting burns my flesh, I feel the wetness between my legs. He rains down another and another on each of my cheeks. The pain and pleasure shoot directly to my clit. It tingles, and I find myself begging for more. Lifting my ass up, I wait for the next one, but it doesn't come.

"This will hurt." That's all he promises before tugging my panties down to my thighs. The lash of leather licks the now sensitive skin of my ass, and it feels as if it's on fire as he continues, and I'm certain from the burn my flesh is now bright red. "Tell me to stop, Peyton," he pleads, almost pained, and I don't know why, because even though my body is trembling from the lashing, my core is pulsing with yearning to be filled. My eyes are shut so tight I see white behind the lids.

"I want you inside me," I find myself uttering, asking him for more pain, for more pleasure. For something I never thought I'd want. And he delivers. His hands grip the stinging globes, massaging them tenderly, then delivering another swat and another until I lose count. Until my nails are digging into the wood. When he finally drops the belt, he tugs my panties all the way down.

I turn to look at him over my shoulder. His eyes are so shot now they're almost black. Dark desire swirls in their depths like a bottomless pit dragging me into the abyss. *The savage*. I don't look away as he shoves his jeans along with his boxers down those muscled thighs. He positions himself at my core, wet and slippery, needy for him.

"Is this how you want your innocence taken?" he asks, and I realize this is it. He's not taking; he's giving me the choice. "Peyton, you have to tell me." He's right. It's my decision. I can't answer him. The words are stuck in my throat. His hand moves then. He jerks himself fast. The tip of his cock grazing over my ass, and then he grunts. Jets of warmth spray over me as he marks me like a feral animal.

"Please, Carrick," I beg. I plead with him, and he nods. He drops to his knees with his body still shaking. Opening me to his gaze, he leans in and laps at me, licking my sodden core. The sensations cause my knees to buckle. He moves so slowly I feel like screaming. Inch by inch, he slips his hot tongue into my quivering entrance. "Fuck," I groan as he fucks me with his tongue, slowly and gently.

A finger dips into me, then he drags it up to my puckered hole. He teases me open, slipping the digit into me, causing me to tense. "Breathe, Kitten. I won't hurt you." It's a promise, and I know he won't. I trust him. He continues to suckle on my clit, his teeth bearing down, causing my body to pulse. I'm so damn close. "That's it. Let go."

I do. I close my eyes and lose myself in the pleasure of his fingers, tongue, and mouth. My release grips me in its earth-shattering hold, and I drench his tongue in my juices. He stops all movement, slipping his finger from my ass, he rises.

"You're delicious," he tells me, helping me to my feet. When I turn to meet his eyes, I feel his cock jutting out once more.

"I want you to take me. To fuck me." My words are filled with honesty, need, and desire.

"Peyton, I—"

"Carrick," I utter his name, peeking up at him under my lashes. "I want it." I've never been surer of anything in my life. I reach out, my hand gripping the smooth, velvety shaft. I stroke him gently, watching his eyes blaze with hunger.

"Go to your bedroom. I'm not taking your virginity on a desk." His order causes me to giggle. "Something funny, Kitten?" he questions, lifting an eyebrow at me. His mouth tilts into a smirk. His accent, thick, broad English, makes everything south of my belly button tingle.

"No." One word, and I release him from my grip. When I turn, he grips my hip, holding me steady before I can disappear and wipes my back with his shirt. Then he releases me, and I walk into the bedroom where I've been lying thinking about him all night. Now he's here, and I can't wait to experience him. All of him. He follows me not long after, his eyes taking in everything surrounding us.

"On the bed. Kneel. Sit back on your heels, and place your hands on your thighs, palms up." His order is gruff. I quickly shuffle onto the bed, posing for him as he requested. I watch him shove off his jeans and boxers. We're both naked. Bared to the other. "You're sure you want this, Kitten?" Once again, he asks me something I nod to. "Words."

"Yes, Sir," I utter my response, which causes him to shudder with yearning. Longing dances in his honeyed eyes. He stalks toward me. Inspecting my position, he nods.

"On your back. Open your legs with your feet on each edge of the mattress. I want to see if you're a dirty girl." I obey. Lying on the plush comforter, I open my legs obscenely, which offers him a view of my wet pussy. "Play with yourself."

"I've—"

"Do not answer me. I said touch your pretty little pussy, Pet." I reach between my legs. Tentatively, I stroke my slick juices, wetting my fingers and allowing them to open the lips of my pussy. Carrick growls at the sight, his fist holding onto his cock so tight I'm sure he's going to pull it off. Watching a man as beautiful and virile as he is only serves to turn me on more. His chiseled body. Dips and peaks of his beautiful stomach are illuminated in the moonlight.

I continue teasing myself. Using my other hand, I

circle my clit with my index finger. My whimpers echo along with Carrick's grunts. He's rock-solid, and I'm drenched and ready.

"Please, I need you," I whimper like a slut. I'm not sure where this has come from, but my body is aching. Pain so acute it's causing me to scoot nearer to him. When he finally steps closer, he positions the crown of his cock at my entrance.

"Don't move. It's going to hurt," he tells me, slipping into my body inch my torturous inch. I don't move. Instead, I grip the sheet with both my hands, fisting the material. I know from taking him down my throat he's big, but the way he fills me is something else. My body stretches for him, taking him deep inside my heat.

The heaviness causes me to wince when he reaches my hymen, but I bite down on my lip to keep from crying out. I don't want him to stop. He is deliciously thick, making me moan when he fully seats himself inside me. Then he starts moving, sliding out and back in. He takes his time, his hands gripping my hips in a vise hold.

His fingers dig into the flesh as he holds me still. When he opens his eyes again they glower. His head drops back, and his grunts are feral and animalistic as they fall from his lips.

"Fuck, you feel so good," he says on a hissed moan. Again and again, he pistons into me. His hips moving faster, back and forth, slamming me into the mattress as he loses all control and fucks me. My thighs tremble as my body tightens.

The pain is gone. All that's left is pleasure as he uses me. As much as he drives pleasure into me, I tighten myself around him. I'm full, filled to the brink. My knuckles turn white. My mewls play alongside his groans.

I feel my release closing in. It's threatening, it's menacing, and when he reaches down to pinch my throbbing bundle of nerves, I fall over the edge.

I scream his name, over and over again. I chant it. I use it as a prayer. He's my god, and I'm on my knees, worshiping him, needing him. Falling. Dropping into his darkness, and I know as he empties his seed inside me, I'll never be free of him.

Our breaths are ragged as he slowly slips from my pussy. The motion causes me to wince, but the pleasured-pain is something I revel in. His gaze is on me, on every part of me. It's something I don't think I could ever get used to. Mainly because the last time someone looked at me like that I was shattered beyond belief. My eyes fall to his cock. It's wet with both our releases as well as my innocence that's been stripped from me. I gave it freely. I wanted it to be him, and it was.

"Was that my first lesson?" I ask, watching him with curiosity. When he doesn't respond, I tip my head to the side, meeting his intense stare.

He opens his mouth then shuts it. Moving around the space, he tugs his jeans and boxers back up, tucking himself away. His shirt is on the floor. I don't even remember him removing it. With controlled precision, he takes the leather belt that licked my skin only moments ago and feeds it into the loops of his jeans.

"It was. You passed it well," he finally utters. He doesn't look at me as he says it, but I can tell he's at war with himself from the rigidness of his shoulders.

"You're leaving?" I ask, pushing off the bed, taking a step closer to him on my wobbly knees. Scarily, I need to be near him. There's something intoxicating about him, something that draws me in. Pulls me closer. There's the danger. That uncontrollable need of wanting someone will only hurt me when he pushes me away into the arms of someone else.

"I have to. I told you, this isn't a relationship, Kitten. It's merely an arrangement. Once we're done, you'll move on, and so will I. You asked me to take your innocence, which I did." He shrugs his shirt on as he says this making his way into the living room and I follow. Somehow, I don't believe a word he's saying.

"You did, and I did. My misunderstanding," I say in agreement, but the words taste bitter on my tongue. Quickly, I grab my panties from the floor and tug them on. Heading to the bar in the far corner of the room, I busy myself with pouring a glass of wine. I know there's no way I can sleep after what just happened. There's a tinge of pain between my thighs. I can feel our desire dripping from me, wetting my already soaked panties.

As I sip the cool liquid, his body heat cocoons me. "Are you okay?" His hands land on my arms as his fingers stroke my skin. "You need to tell me if I've been too harsh, or if you're at your limit. I . . ." His words taper off, and when I turn to him, I meet those beautiful eyes shimmering with hints of chocolate.

"You're . . .?"

"I'm not used to this. Mason is the trainer. Me . . . I'm . . . I don't know." He shakes his head almost sadly, and I wonder what could've happened to him to make him so cold, so detached.

"The asshole?" I ask, giggling when his mouth tilts into a smirk. It's playful, so different to the emotions that swirled around us moments ago.

"Yes. I suppose you might call me that. Taking your virginity like that, I'm . . . sorry. I've always been cold. It's the only way I can survive." There's no apology in his words. He knows what he's like, and he doesn't want me to believe differently. Honesty. I've not had that with anyone before. My life is a lie. All I've ever known are things that have been made up. It's ingrained inside me, so deep, so fucking deep I'll never get them out. Secrets.

"Or perhaps you're only acting that way because you don't want me to feel more about this," I tell him, stalking around him, needing air. His scent is intoxicating. He makes my chest ache, my heart hurt, and mostly, he makes me want more. And this between us is far too intense for me to put down as merely fun.

"No, Peyton. I am an asshole. And not the kind you read about in books, not the kind that will change for the right woman." The no-nonsense tone causes me to nod in agreement. It's clear what this is. So, I smile, plastering it on my face like I was taught to. Lies.

"You made that abundantly clear, Carrick. I don't expect you to ever walk in here with a ring. So please, don't think I'm that kind of girl. I never have been, and I never will be."

"Good. Then we're on the same page," he responds easily, but his shoulders are rigid with tension. He turns and makes his way to my door. The apartment is small, compared to the usual standards I'm used to, but I just needed escape.

"We are."

Two words, and he's out the door without so much as a goodbye. I release a breath I was holding for the longest time and slump against the wall. Without him in the same vicinity, my brain is clear.

This agreement may be the end of my heart. Day by

day, I know I'll fall for him. I've had the worst taste in men, and I've already signed the contract. Even though I don't know how I'll get through it, I want to. But I don't admit why I really want it. I can't. Because voicing the words are worse than what just happened between us.

NINE

CARRICK

Peyton Moore.

I ordered a background check on her, and it seems she's hidden within the system of paperwork and bullshit. He didn't find anything incriminating. The problem is, he didn't find anything at all. I expected results, but for some reason, she's clean. It doesn't matter who it is in my life, I always make sure I know who I'm getting into bed with, so to speak. Especially when it's something long term.

When I asked Savannah, she's not been too forthcoming about her best friend either. I always get what I want. I've grown up with everything I need at my fingertips, and as much as Peyton has proved a challenge, I'm not scared off. I want more.

I don't blame Savannah though. I told her that this

is nothing more than an arrangement, but I'm lying to myself if I believe last night hasn't done something to me. It's fucked with my head, and I don't know how to deal with it.

This woman who's walked into my life and consumed my every thought is a mystery, and even though I shouldn't make an exception, being who I am, I no longer care. All I want is her.

When my office door opens, I look up to find Mason staring at me. My partner and friend. He's the only one, besides Oliver, who knows who I really am. When I first arrived, he took me in and made sure my life got back on track. When we opened Sins together, I knew there was no one else I could put my trust in.

"You're going through with it?" he asks, stalking into the space, shutting the door behind him. Leaning back in my chair, I nod. He doesn't need to know my motivation to take Peyton on. We may be best friends, but there are some things I like to keep to myself when it comes to my submissives. Even though he knows I fuck a lot of women, I can't tell him the real reason Peyton has jarred me so much.

"I didn't think I needed your permission."

"You don't," he says, settling himself in the seat opposite my desk. There's nothing left to say, but I know Mason, and this is not something he's going to let go. I don't blame him. I'm not a long-term Dominant. Never have been. After what happened with Aurora, I have never had an inkling to take on anyone in my life. Allowing myself a situation to even utter the words *I own you* does not present itself to me any longer. It's easier to indulge in playtime, and then move on.

"But?" I ask, knowing he's waiting to say something more. He drags his gaze over to the wall of toys, implements I use on the toys who enter my office asking for it.

"I don't know, Carrick. You tell me." He turns his gaze back to me. "This isn't like you, and it intrigues me." The corner of his mouth lifts an inch as he regards me with a smile. Curiosity clear on his features.

"Well it shouldn't, Mason. There's nothing to tell. She's beautiful, she asked me to train her, and I agreed. You're reading too much into this." I hope he'll drop it because I can't give him more than that. Even though

I know where he's coming from. I know why he's so confused, so *intrigued*. It's been years since I've even looked at a blonde woman, let alone a submissive.

"I've known you far too long to believe your bullshit," he counters easily. "And I know when you're lying too, Rick. The last time you were this caught up in a woman was Eva. But, you see, what I don't get" --he says, leaning his elbows on his knees-- "never, and I mean never, have I seen you with a blonde. Not a toy, not a sub that's walked in here asking for you. So . . ." His words trail off into tense silence, leaving me guarded. He's close. Too fucking close. "Who was she, Rick?" And there it is. The question I knew Mason would ask. I knew he'd figure it out.

"What makes you ask that?"

"Don't bullshit me, Rick. I'm not stupid. I know there must be a reason behind what you do. There always is, and something tells me you've been burned. Tell me how? And why now suddenly do you take on a woman like Peyton. Who is she a ghost of?"

Pushing up from my chair, I stalk toward the bar and pour a double shot of Scotch. Downing it in one gulp, I turn to Mason. "This isn't something I talk about, man. The past stays where I leave it. Behind me."

"Tell me, Carrick. If you're doing this to get some sort of closure, that's fucked up. Peyton doesn't need you to use her for your sick games." He's right. I nod.

"What if she was using me as much as I am her? Did you ever think of that? Yes, she may be innocent to this life, but Peyton Moore is hiding something, and I intend finding out exactly what it is." He doesn't respond, merely glares at me with those dark green eyes that seem black in this low light.

"You know, all these years I've known you, I never pegged you for a masochist." He sighs, rising from the seat, stalking toward me. He grabs a tumbler and pours himself a drink. Clinking his glass on mine, he lifts it to his lips and downs it in one swallow.

"What makes you say that?" I question, turning toward the window overlooking the club. There, sitting in the corner booth, are Peyton and Savannah. They're giggling like school girls, and I wonder if she's told her friend I took her virginity last night.

"You've spent eight years avoiding the ghost you

were running from, but now you're walking straight into hell holding her hand," he utters from beside me as he sees his girl with Peyton. "You know, Rick, there's a time to let go of the past and move on to a new future. Perhaps I am wrong. Maybe this girl will drag you out of the self-destruct you've been on for so long."

"Only one thing will ensure I let the past go, Mason. And that vengeance is coming soon. As for Peyton, she's a toy I'm training. Nothing more." My words are cold, devoid of emotion, because if I allow myself just an inkling of what she's making me feel, I'll break.

Mason doesn't say any more. Instead, he pats me on the shoulder and leaves. I'm alone with my thoughts. With the fear that Peyton Moore is going to unravel me. And I can't do a damn thing about it.

Stalking into the club, I find Mason and Savvie sitting at the bar. It's still early, but there are a few people in the booths. As I reach them, my best friend's green gaze lands on my gold one. He leans in, planting a kiss on Savannah's forehead, but his stare is on me all the time.

"Mason," I smirk, knocking once on the bar to get Dylan's attention. He knows what I want. A gin and tonic. It's the only drink I have when I'm down in the club. "Savvie, looking beautiful as ever." She turns her attention to me. Her big sapphire eyes look up at me.

"Rick, I've missed you." She rises, wrapping me in a hug I don't expect. When I flit my gaze to Mason, he just shrugs.

"And this?" I question her, chuckling as she steps back and smiles.

"Look after my best friend, Anderson, or I'll have your balls," she warns me. She pierces me with a serious stare, and all I can do is nod.

"Of course, I will. I'm not a complete asshole, you know," I whisper in her ear, loud enough to get a snort from Mason.

"Are you going to be around tonight?" Mason asks, his expression filled with worry. If I respond, he'll know where I'll be. But if I don't, there'll be more questions.

"I may stick around. If something comes up, then I

won't be." The glass Dylan poured earlier is empty. He gestures for a refill, but I shake my head. "Later," I say. I'm not a fan of drinking. I've seen too many submissives and Dominants fuck up by getting wasted and heading into the rooms.

I've spent one too many nights pulling them out of there and having to ban them for life. Even though there are contracts in place ensuring they can't sue, I feel like shit for it because I've lost the client.

When I reach my office, I push open the door and stop dead in my tracks. On the floor, kneeling like the perfect submissive is Peyton. She's dressed in a white corset that has pink ribbons threaded through creating a zigzag pattern. Her tits are covered, but they're barely contained in the tight fabric.

Her head is bowed. Her lashes flutter, and I know she's aware of me. As she should be. Her legs are spread beautifully, and the scrap of material covering her cunt is taunting from between her thighs. Both her hands are behind her back. I've seen women kneel for me many times. I've allowed them to present themselves to me, but never has a woman new to this life ever captured my attention like Peyton.

"You're early," I say, finding my voice in the shock still evident in my tone. She doesn't respond. Instead, she stays silent, just like I expected her to. I haven't directly asked her a question, so there's no need for her to acknowledge me. Stepping into the office, I shut the door with a gentle click.

Her perfume, the scent of a rare orchid, invades my senses. She is a delicate flower amongst this darkness that will only tear her apart, petal by petal. All the men downstairs are not good enough for her. And as much as I don't want to admit it, neither am I.

"Eyes up." She obeys. Her big jade eyes meet mine. They shine with excitement and yearning. I shouldn't be training her, but I can't help myself. Her obedience is more than intoxicating. It's addictive. "You look beautiful, Kitten," I tell her with a smile.

A soft blush paints her cheeks, and she offers me an innocent grin. "Thank you, Sir."

I'm not a sadist, but I want to mark her more than I have anyone else before. Even Aurora. I shouldn't do it. Her training shouldn't be met with harsh punishments, even after last night when I lost all fucking control. But deep in my gut, all I want to do is see her creamy skin that reminds me of porcelain marred with beautiful red welts.

I have a plan of what I'll be offering her tonight. I thought about it earlier, and it's got me hard already. Knowing she'll experience all of this for the first time with me is heady. For some reason, I want all her firsts with me. When I left her last night and walked into my apartment still marked in her bloody innocence, I jerked off again and again, and even seeing her in my sanctuary right now, I know I can't allow her to walk away from me. I don't want to be rid of her.

I don't say anything. Instead, I walk over to my desk, set down my phone and keys, and shrug off my jacket. She's silent. Beautiful. Fucking perfect.

All my life, I was in love with one woman. My heart had molded itself to hers, and I believed I'd never feel that way about anyone again. Perhaps I won't. Agreed, this is not a relationship, but my feelings for Peyton are completely different.

Ten

Peyton

"Stand for me, Kitten," he utters in a tone drenched in lust. I rise to my feet. The lingerie I bought earlier today feels exquisite against my skin. Carrick stalks around me, silently taking me in. Every inch of my exposed skin tingles with anticipation of what's to come. "I'd like to take you to my apartment tonight," he informs me when he stops in front of me.

"Okay, Sir," I tell him easily. The words fluid on my tongue. He smiles with satisfaction clear on his handsome face. Stepping behind his desk, he shuts his laptop off and grabs a set of keys. He takes his suit jacket from the back of his black leather office chair and drapes it over my shoulders. His scent, spicy and warm, wraps around me.

"Can't have anyone seeing what's mine," he says,

murmuring the words in my ear. He leads me out of the office and down a long, dark hallway. We reach a small elevator, which we take silently to the top floor of the building. As soon as the doors slide open, we step out into a private corridor that has a faint scent of orchids.

"This is yours?" I ask, trailing my fingertips over the petals of a bright pink flower. Orchids are beautiful, rare because they're so difficult to grow.

"I love things that aren't easily found." Carrick's voice carries a hint of something. I can't pinpoint it just then, but he's gripped my attention more than anyone ever has. "Come, Kitten." He ushers me inside his apartment.

The space is elegant. Nothing I'd pictured it would be. Slate gray walls are adorned by intricate modern art. Two large pillars of open brick offset the living room. The floor-to-ceiling windows with their black frames overlooking the city are draped by flowing cream curtains which don't look like they close.

There are two large sofas, both a rich magenta—dark, luxurious pink. A black shag rug sits under a glass-top table, and a modern fireplace overlooks the scene.

It's open plan, and the kitchen to my right is black and chrome, with hints of color coming from the cabinet doors. A fine pattern of the same pink adorns the seating.

"Do you like it?" Carrick asks after my perusal of his apartment lands back on him. The low lights that sit flush in the ceiling glow a soft cream, which turns the contours of Rick's face from human to a statue carved from marble, and my fingers itch to touch him.

"It's beautiful. I didn't pin you for an art lover," I tell him, padding toward the one piece of an abstract woman, sitting with her back to the viewer. She's naked, and the curve of her spine is a perfect slight S, giving way to the white sheet she's sitting on, which hints at her bare ass. Her hair is pinned atop her head, with thin tendrils which frame her delicate neck.

"Those are all Mason's work," he tells me. I'm shocked, because I had no idea. Savannah has never mentioned his art to me. I was clueless Mason even knew how to hold a paintbrush, let alone create such beautiful paintings.

"I didn't know."

Carrick joins me, his body cocooning me from

behind. His body heat calms my erratic heartbeat as he slips the jacket from my shoulders. His hands on my shoulders steady me as he holds me in place. The gentle kiss he places on my neck causes goosebumps to rise in its wake.

There's never been a time I've been surer of what I want. The man I want. Every suitor my father brought to the house was after one thing--our money. They saw me as the innocent little girl. Not wife material. And I didn't prove them otherwise. I didn't want to be paraded around like a trophy. Deep down, I needed to feel wanted, desired. A woman, and not a girl.

Carrick gives me that in spades, and I've not been around him for very long. He's offered me the one thing I most desired. To feel beautiful. When I first thought about submission, it wasn't about the sex. I believed it was about the emotion that comes from it. Kneeling for one man, allowing him to offer you pleasure is not a weakness. There's a strength in it. When I waited for him in the office, I felt real for the first time in years. Knowing I'm the one who holds the power, because if I don't allow him to spank me, fuck me, he can't take it.

He reaches for my hair, his fist gripping the wavy tendrils. With a harsh tug, my head falls back against his chest, and a whimper of need tumbles from my mouth. This man will be my undoing, unraveling me bit by bit until all that's left is my need for him.

"Come, Kitten," he orders, turning me to face him. His fingers lift my chin gently, forcing me to lift my gaze to his. "Tonight, we'll learn how you enjoy different sensations." His words elicit a tingle that trickles down my spine. My body is already trembling with anticipation at the thought of what he's going to do to me.

"What do you mean?" My brow furrows in confusion.

"Have you ever heard about or read about sensation play?" he asks, as if teaching a small child. I guess I am. Each step I take into his world is another learning curve, and if I have to be honest, I'm excited.

"Not really," I answer honestly. If there's one thing I know it's that I need to tell him how I'm feeling or what I'm experiencing for this to work.

"Okay, let's go to my bedroom. If you feel out of your depth and need to use your safe word, then you do it at any time. Do you understand me, Peyton?"

"Yes, Sir," I murmur, teasing him with the words that seem to turn his eyes molten. It looks like liquid gold trickling through the depths of his gaze.

"Good girl." Carrick slips his hand in mine and leads me down a long hallway into a bedroom the size of my apartment. It's massive.

The opulence of his bedroom is breathtaking. A king-sized bed sits against a brick wall. The headboard is made of tufted velvet. Black sheets adorn the bed with pillow cases the same dark magenta as the sofa. Four steel posts sit on each corner of the bed, and I know what they're used for before I notice the leather cuffs locked to them.

Two large pink orchids sit on either of the jet-colored nightstands. The carpet is thick, plush under my bare feet and the color of ash.

Once again, I'm greeted with floor-to-ceiling windows with the same view as the living room.

"This is . . ." I can't find words to describe the bedroom.

"I'm glad you like it. I want you on the bed, Kitten.

On your back. I'll be binding you to the four posts," he tells me easily, strolling over to the window, oozing confidence like it's a cologne. I move quickly, finding that the sheets are cool against my skin. The silky material is delicate and shiny. I lie back, unsure of what I'm doing. He doesn't move, merely stands looking out over the view with his arms folded in front of his chest. He's still dressed in his blue shirt and black slacks.

I take a moment to admire him. Over six feet of lean muscle. His hair, the color of warm chestnuts, sits messily atop his head. His profile of a chiseled jaw, sharp features, and his softly tanned skin gives the illusion that he's perfect. Beautiful.

But I know no person is perfect. We all have flaws.

"Close your eyes, Kitten," he tells me without turning. I shut them immediately, and that's when the anticipation kicks in. Silence echoes loudly in the darkened room. My skin skitters with a cool shiver when I try to picture where he is, or if he's moving. I can't hear anything, but that doesn't mean he hasn't perhaps shifted on the spot.

A shuffle of material sounds like a foghorn to my

ears.

"If you open your eyes, I'll whip your ass. Do you understand me?"

"Yes, Sir," I purr like the kitten he calls me. More shuffling of material, and then I feel his hand on my ankle, the cold leather wraps around it like an ominous sign.

"Breathe, Peyton. I won't hurt you." His assurance eases my tension somewhat. I've never been tied up before. But then again, I'd never been spanked, and I loved it. He continues to bind me to the four corners of his bed. I'm spread open to his gaze. "You look beautiful against the darkness, my sweet little Kitten." I can't help smiling.

"Perhaps I'm your light." I don't know where the words come from, but the air in the room shifts. It changes as soon as the last word falls from my mouth.

"Perhaps." It's the only response. He's not angry, I can tell, but he sounds almost pained by the prospect. His soft footfalls on the carpet are now as loud as if they were on tiles. When he returns to me, soft material covers my eyes. "Lift your head," he orders. Once the blindfold is in place, he rises from the bed, and then I'm once again met with silence.

"Carrick?"

He doesn't respond. My heart patters in my chest, but then it leaps into my throat when I feel a gentle caress on my left foot. It's light, almost tentative.

"What is that?" I ask in confusion, but he doesn't tell me. The sensation trails up my leg to my thigh and over the corset. I know this because soon it reaches my face, and that's when I realize it's a feather.

"Do you like this corset, Kitten?" he asks.

"Why?"

He chuckles in response to my question. The feather disappears, then, moments later, I hear a strange sound I can't place. Once the corset falls way from my torso, I realize he cut the ribbons holding it in place. Gently, he tugs the now ruined lingerie out from under me.

"It was in my way," he says nonchalantly. Once again, the feather is back, tickling its way over my stomach, ribs, then my sensitive nipples. They harden into peaks, aching for a harsher touch than he's offering. "So pretty." His adoration causes my cheeks to heat, presumably in a blush.

He pulls away, moving around the room, and I wonder what I'm in store for next. Moments pass, and I'm lying in darkness and silence. When I hear his footfalls again, another sound I can't place causes me to shiver in apprehension.

"No fear in this room. I'll never hurt you, Kitten." His voice is right at my ear, so soft and gentle it calms me immediately. He moves away, his hot breath gone, then I hear it. A strike of a match sounds around me, echoing in my ears. The scent of orchids and lavender fills the room. "This is going to tingle," he informs me before the sensations of what I can only imagine is hot wax trickles over my bare skin. A straight line from my knee to my upper thigh, getting close to my pussy but never reaching the now-slick entrance of my body.

Once both legs are warm and sensitive, he does the same over my stomach. The movements so slow, I inhale a sharp breath, awaiting the moment they reach my nipples. When they do, I cry out. My back arches in response. I've never felt such pleasured-pain. As soon as the wax cools, he continues to pour more hot liquid on my breasts, seconds before it has time to cool, an ice-cold sensation shoots through me. From the heat at my legs, I know Carrick is straddling me.

He doesn't speak, but the ice cube screams volumes. He's using his mouth. Goose bumps rise on every inch of my flesh. Once he's run out of the icy block, he grabs another from a glass to my left and continues his ministrations down to my now-drenched core.

The water trickles over me. Whimpers and mewls fall from my lips. I beg and plead for him to do something, touch me, kiss me, fuck me, but he doesn't respond. He doesn't even move. The bed dips as he moves. Once I'm alone again, I turn my head, but it's pointless, I can't see a thing.

"You're exquisite. You know, Kitten, I'm breaking every rule with you." His words hold raw honesty. I'm not sure what he means, but I can't ask him because suddenly wet material is shoved into my mouth. "Can you taste that, baby?" he murmurs. "That's your sweet little cunt." I can. I try to nod, and he chuckles. He removes the panties.

"Sir," I whimper, my voice raspy and low. "I need . .

. Can you . . . I mean . . ."

"Do you need to come, Kitten?" I picture his face, and I know for a fact he's sitting or standing there smirking like the confident asshole he is.

"Please." He loves me begging. I know he does.

"I have five rules, Peyton," he informs me without giving me an ounce of what I need. He doesn't touch me, but I feel a feather light stroke over my flesh. "I don't take on submissives. I never play a scene with a sub more than once. I never allow them into my bedroom." It's then I feel the lick of leather. It feels as if there are a million fingers touching me. "I never allow emotion into my scenes or with the women I fuck." It's gone as quickly as it arrives, and then the bite attacks with vengeance.

"Carrick!" I cry out when he lashes my thighs, my calves, moving higher he attacks my stomach, my breasts. When a stray strand of leather licks at my pussy it turns my body molten. I'm drenched. More so than I've ever been before.

"My sweet little virgin," he taunts. He took that, he took my body, and right now he has my mind in his commanding grip. He continues his assault. It wracks me violently. My body aches, tenses, trembles. I'm so close. I feel an orgasm tightening my core. It feels as if a fist has me in its hold, and I have no way of stopping the onslaught. The leather causes the wax to fly off my body, and I'm once again bare.

"I'm going . . . Oh god, Carrick, please, please?"

He lashes me on my mound. "In this room, in a scene, it's Sir," he commands, and I try to nod but my body is not my own. It's his. I've handed it to him, and I have no way of getting it back because I don't want to.

A thud on the carpet tells me he's dropped the whip or flogger or whatever he was using. Suddenly, his body is on me, between my thighs, and he drives inside me in one long stroke.

"I knew you were needy for me, Kitten, but you're fucking drenched," he grunts in my ear. His voice is ragged, husky as he moves inside me. He's thick, hard, and he stretches me almost painfully. He doesn't give me a moment to get used to his cock, because his hips move, faster, slamming me into the bed. I can't move. I can't touch him. Everything is too much. Sensations skitter through me. Electric currents blaze through my veins. My blood is boiling, turning my core molten, and my toes curl when he pumps into my tight entrance.

I feel my own juices dripping from me. "Come for me. I need to feel it, Peyton." He murmurs my name. His mouth latches onto an exposed nipple, sucking it hard into his warm, wet mouth. His teeth graze the hardened bud, biting down hard, and I lose all control.

My head thrashes into the mattress, my keening cry reminding me of a goddamn banshee. I tug on my restraints, but I have nowhere to go. My toes curl into the sheets. He doesn't let up. He continues his thrusts deep into my cunt, ensuring I'm drained of everything I have to give him.

My throat burns. He drives in one last time, jerking as his body releases hot seed deep inside me, and I welcome every drop. I'm his. There's no doubt this man owns more than just my body. And that scares me shitless.

Eleven

Carrick

The way her body curls into the sheets is erotic and alluring. The curves of her in the sliver of light give off a sensual vision. I wish I could capture her just like that, in this moment. She's incredibly beautiful. The way she took everything I gave her and begged for more only had my mind cementing the thought she's mine.

It's been such a long time since I've even thought of a woman spending more than one night in my bed. I've broken all my rules. The only thing is, I haven't told her the last one.

I have five rules.

I broke every single last one of them.

The fifth is the most important.

And slowly, but surely, I've shattered that one into tiny fragments.

I rise, padding into the living room to find reprieve from the smell of sex in my bedroom. There's never been a doubt in my mind that I couldn't walk away from this, but, Peyton has found a way into my head.

The silence hangs heavy around me, taunting and teasing. The truth of who I am is still a secret to her. I haven't told her who I really am or what I've done. She also has no idea that the woman in my past, the one person I loved more than life, could be her twin.

I can't explain why I haven't told her. There's no way I can. If she finds out, she'll walk out, and the thought of that hurts my chest more than I care to admit. More than I should allow myself to feel. Mason was right; I was an idiot for believing I was in command.

As much as I am the dominant in this relationship, she's the one who is ultimately owning me. I've been topped from the bottom without noticing it. And the woman who's in my bed is unaware of how much power she really does hold over me.

Lifting the tumbler to my lips, I take a long drink of the gin and tonic. The harsh, bitter liquid trickles down my throat, and I revel in the burn. The silence of the dark night is what I need to figure out what I'm doing. My mind is awash with her. Everything about her, the sweet scent, the intoxicating flavor, and the way she offers me her all. She doesn't hold back. It's dangerous. Because soon, I'll be addicted to her, and there's no way I can go back from that.

My sister arrives in a few days, I knew my father wouldn't want her coming here on her own, so Callan is flying along with her. Having both siblings here will be difficult. The three O'Leary kids back together again. All the memories, everything I've long since buried, will once again be dug up, and I don't think I'm ready for it.

I look forward to seeing them both, but deep down, I'm just not sure the memory of Aurora will be hidden from Peyton. Lies are the only things I hate. Hiding something from a woman I'm starting to care about is something I'd rather not do, but I don't know if I have a choice.

"You're so quiet, Little Kitten," I murmur over the rim of my glass, not turning to meet her gaze. I felt her moments ago, those green eyes piercing through my armor. The scent of her is everywhere, and I know even if I sent her home right now, nothing will rid me of her.

I realize it was stupid of me to think I could take on a submissive, train her, and let her go. Not because I couldn't do it, but the realization that I'm holding on to Peyton because she looks like Aurora hit me an hour ago. When I opened my eyes and saw her sleeping beside me, I knew my heart is no longer safe.

"I woke up and you were gone," she tells me. Her soft footfalls are the only sound as she moves silently toward me. A gentle touch on my shoulder burns through me. Her skin, warm, silky smooth, ignites my blood.

"I had to think," I tell her, gulping down the last of my drink, not meeting her inquisitive gaze.

Her innocence is something I can't deny turns me on. Perhaps that's why I can't say no, why I can't walk away from her.

"Are you pondering ways to tell me to leave?"

Her question stills me for a moment before I turn to regard her. Green eyes shimmer in the low light. The small, delicate smile on her lips makes me want to kiss her, to devour those whimpers she gifts me each time

I'm near her.

There's nothing I want more than to take her and make her mine, but I can't.

"I was thinking about how life has fucked me over time and again," I confess.

"And you decided a drink in the dark is what will quell your anger?" she asks, perching herself on the arm of the sofa beside me. She's wrapped in white cotton. My shirt I was wearing earlier draped over her skin. It looks better on her than it does me.

"I don't know, Peyton. I'm not an easy man to be with." I shrug. Once again all I give her is honesty. There's nothing for me to hide from this girl because I know she sees my truth.

"Nobody is easy to be with, Carrick," she says, rising and stepping around to stand before me. Her frame silhouetted by the darkened window makes her look ethereal. "We all have darkness inside us. Nobody is perfect, but it's not about that. It's about finding the person you're imperfect with and allowing them to love you the way you are."

Her words wash over me. Calming my breathing

and the thoughts running through my mind. With a sigh, I set the glass down and rise. My hands come up to cup her face. My thumb swipes over her lower lip that's plump and begging to be devoured.

I allow myself to lower my mouth to hers. I want this girl more than I thought was possible. My heart, however, is torn. I plant a kiss on her lips, with my hands trailing down her body. Finding her hips, I tug her closer.

When she whimpers, I turn feral. My tongue darts out, fighting for entry into her body, which she allows me. As if I'm always meant to be there. I kiss her hard, abandoning all the earlier fears, I revel in her flavor. Her taste is sweet, delicate like an orchid. She's the ultimate prize, but I don't know if I'm worthy of winning.

Her hands twine themselves around my neck, and my palms find her pert ass. Lifting her against me, I stalk toward the panes of the window and pin her between the glass and my body. She gasps as the cold seeps through the material of my shirt. My hips roll against her, my cock pressing against her warmth.

"Rick," she murmurs, causing me to halt my attack on her flesh. "I need you inside me," she whimpers. Her gaze pleading with me to take her. Shoving my boxers down, I grip my cock and tease her with the tip. The fact that she came in here without panties on isn't lost on me.

She came to seduce.

To taunt.

I stare at her as I sink into her cunt, slow and torturous. Her eyes widen with every inch. She pulls her bottom lip between her pearly white teeth, and she bites down when I fully seat myself inside her.

"You're a tease," I tell her. The corner of my mouth kicking up into a smirk when she giggles. It's a light, melodic sound.

"You're a glutton," she retorts. I pull out and slam back in, eliciting a moan from her mouth. I move faster, but not enough to give her the release she needs.

Her eyes glaze over. "Carrick, please." Her plea falls in the space between us. I fit inside her like I was made to. Her body fits around me like a glove, sucking me into her heat, wanting more. I indulge in her, my mouth crashing into the curve of her neck. The smooth flesh tastes like temptation, like promises, and I wonder just how long this will last.

Her nails claw my shoulders as my hips piston against her. My cock throbbing as I drive into her wet hole. Her moans are beautiful, erotic.

"Carrick," she utters my name on a melody of desire and lust. Hunger thick in her voice as I roll my hips, causing my shaft to hit that spot inside her that has her body shuddering and pulsing. The tightness of her around me is too much, and I'm barely holding onto restraint.

"I want you, Kitten. I want all of you." My honesty is raw. My words feather over her, sending her reeling as an orgasm shatters through her slim body. Her pussy pulses, taking me along with her, and we both tumble over the precipice of desire.

Her eyes flutter open. Long lashes sweep across her cheeks as she blinks away the high. I can't stop watching her. Seeing her pleasure is like a drug--I need it. And I want to be the one responsible for her orgasms.

I can't fight it anymore. I don't want to.

"That was . . .," she murmurs, her words falling silent as she attempts finding something to describe the connection. Nothing can. I believe Peyton has walked into my life for a reason.

At first, I thought it was because she could offer me closure. But I realize now that's not it. She's not here to make me stop caring. Her presence in my life is to allow me to feel again. Affection was never on my list of things to do. Allowing myself to care about anyone else but Rory was something I could never fathom, but that's changed.

"It was real," I tell her.

The air shifts between us. Her legs are wrapped around me. I'm still inside her, hard as if I'd never come at all. My release, mixed with hers, drips from her body. She smiles when I lie her on the black rug. Her body open to me. Reaching for the material, I grip the shirt. When I rip it, the buttons fly in every direction, clinking against the window, tiles, and cabinet behind us.

"Carrick," she murmurs, smiling up at me with affection burning into me.

"Peyton, this is--" I start. Leaning in, I plant kisses over her flesh. Taking a nipple into my mouth, I suck it hard. My teeth bite into the hardened bud, causing her to whimper. Her fingers tangle into my hair, tugging me closer. Her hips rise up, her core rubbing against me.

"Please, fuck, Carrick," she mumbles, moans like a sultry temptress.

There's a soft purr that tumbles from her lips as I tease and taunt her nipples. Tugging and tweaking, drawing more pleasure from her body than I ever thought possible. When I finally release her, I sit back, my hand raising and raining down on her to swat on her pussy. Another, and another. Her pink cunt lips are puffy, her clit sensitive, causing her hips to buck with each slap.

"Fuck!" she cries out as her body shudders on the floor. Her thighs shake as her release slams into her. I watch in awe as she let's go. She's perfection.

"You are perfect," I tell her while planting kisses over her smooth, flat stomach. My tongue dips into her belly button, causing her to squirm. Trailing my fingers up her thighs, I splay them wide. When I cast my glance up her body, I find those green eyes staring back at me.

"What are you—?"

I cut her question off with my tongue, lapping at her core, her sweet arousal dripping onto my tongue, and I delve into the tight heat that's so welcoming. Her head drops back, her fingers grip the rug beneath her as I taste our combined releases. The combination is a heady mixture of love and lust.

She lifts from the carpet when my teeth graze her clit, biting down hard to draw out her pleasure and those melodic mewls. She's a kitten, but when she loses control, she's a goddamn lioness. Her golden waves splay on the black carpet, her porcelain skin shimmers with a sheen of sweat, and I lick my way up to her mouth.

"Taste us," I tell her, and she does. Lifting her head, she sucks my tongue into her mouth then moans as if she revels in our flavor as much as I do. Gently, I slide into her once more. I can't stop wanting her, needing to be inside her.

There's nothing more I want than to see and feel every part of her.

Even the part I told her not to give me.

I want her heart too.

TWELVE

PEYTON

A gentle sound stirs me from a dream of sunshine and golden eyes. When I finally move, I roll over to find the bed empty and cold, and I realize he must have been gone for a long while. Sighing, I shuffle up so my back is against the headboard. The ache between my legs reminds me of last night.

We fucked, we made love, and I'm almost certain there was a shift in the emotion between us. As much as I didn't want to, I know deep down I've fallen. The problem is, I don't know if it's for the man or what he does to me. The notion of submission.

I shut my eyes, hoping to quell the confusion in my mind. My heart warring with my rational thinking. I want Carrick, but he said we're not in a relationship. This is merely a contract between two consenting adults.

He made it very clear my heart wasn't what he wanted.

"Good morning, Kitten." His voice comes from the doorway, causing me to snap my eyes to the entrance. There, in all his sensual glory, is Carrick Anderson. Wearing a pair of black sweats that hang low on his taut hips, he looks delicious, which makes my core pulse. How can this man turn me molten without uttering a filthy word?

"Good morning, Sir," I taunt, allowing the sheet to fall, baring my breasts to his hungry stare. The corner of his mouth kicks up, one dark eyebrow arching in question. "I thought you had left," I tell him, shifting onto my knees.

"I made breakfast, but I'd prefer eating in the kitchen," he tells me.

Nodding, I rise from the bed to reach for the robe he set out last night.

"No. I want you naked," he growls with a sinful smirk. Without any more words, he crooks his finger, calling me to him. I obey, following him out the door and down the hallway. The apartment looks so different with the sun streaming through the windows.

My soft footfalls mingle with his, and I can't help grinning at how almost normal this feels. We're like a couple, but not. We don't go on dates, but he gives me pleasure in ways I couldn't imagine. There's no meeting the family, or even just a dinner with friends. It's just us. And I realize I like it.

"What's on your mind, Peyton?" he questions as I slip onto the cold bar stool at the breakfast bar in the center of the kitchen.

"Do you have family?" I question, realizing that's too normal a question for him to answer. His brows crease in confusion at my question, which I must admit does sound strange. "I mean, we've not really spoken about our personal lives. But . . ."

"Yes, I have a brother and a sister," he tells me as he sets a mug of steaming coffee in front of me. "My mother died when I was younger, but my dad is still alive."

"Do they live close by?" I question once more, lifting the coffee to my mouth to take a long sip. The mocha roasted flavor hits my taste buds, and I moan in pleasure.

"England. I came here a few years ago," Carrick

tells me, turning to watch me for a moment. "What about you?" he asks, placing two plates filled with eggs, bacon, mushrooms, and toast between us, and he takes his seat opposite me.

"I have a brother, Chance. He'll be here in a few days. It's the longest we've ever been apart." I smile, thinking about my brother. "My parents were killed in a car accident a few years ago."

"I'm sorry to hear that." Carrick's cool demeanor changes when he looks at me again. His eyes hold affection, and I wonder if it's because I just told him I lost my parents, or because he feels something more for me.

"So, do you like America? I guess you must since you've stayed for so long." I lift the toast, biting into it. The scent of the food makes my stomach growl.

"I think you need to eat." He points toward the plate and in effect shuts off the conversation. He doesn't like talking about his past, or the woman who's no longer in his life, which only makes me more curious.

We eat in silence. The only sound is the clatter of the cutlery on the plates. My eyes snap to Carrick when he rises, but it's only to grab the coffee pot and refill both our mugs. Once he sets it back on the warmer, he joins me once more.

I clear my plate and sit back to find his eyes on me. "What?" I ask, tipping my head to the side.

"I want to take you out. On a date."

"I thought—"

"Peyton," he starts, then sighs. His gaze drops to the mug as he twirls it on the marble counter. As if mesmerized by the movement, he talks to the mug instead of looking at me. "I didn't plan to enjoy you or our time together as much as I do."

"Well, I guess I didn't expect to want to spend time with you either. Carrick, I'm not asking—"

His gaze flits to mine when he interrupts me. "I want to be with you, Peyton. But, this is new to me. It's been a long time since I've been with someone I care about."

His confession causes my heart to stutter then slam against my rib cage. He falls silent, and I wait, holding my breath to see what else he's about to say, but he doesn't continue. Instead, he rises and stalks toward me. Without a word, he lifts me effortlessly in his arms and walks us down the hall toward the bathroom.

He sets me down on the counter and turns on the shower. I watch as he shoves his sweats off and steps out of them. His taut ass is sexy as it leads down to his muscled thighs. When I drag my gaze up toward his face, I find him staring at me with amusement swimming in his golden orbs.

"Enjoying the view?" he questions mischievously. When he's playful, there's an innocence to him, like a little boy.

"Perhaps." I giggle. Jumping off the counter, I step under the spray. I tilt my head to glance at him over my shoulder. "Are you joining me?"

"Perhaps." He throws my response back at me with a chuckle.

Once we're both in the shower, he shuts the glass door and picks up the body wash. Carefully, he squirts a handful onto the sponge and starts washing my back with the sweet-smelling liquid. His touch is gentle, almost loving compared to the way he normally would spank me. He moves down to my ass, then my legs. His hands come up, squeezing the cheeks of my backside, opening me to his stare.

I cast a glance down to where he's kneeling and watch as he rinses the soap suds off. As soon as I'm clean, he teases the hole with his finger. The sensation causes my knees to buckle, and I'm clawing at the tiles when his tongue flicks over the forbidden entrance.

A moan slips from my mouth when he slowly pushes one digit into me, fingering my ass. He works it in and out, then another slips into me. Scissoring me open, he moves tentatively. My body trembles as sensations of pleasure and a hint of pain shoot through every inch of me.

"Rick," I utter when his tongue laps at my pussy while he fingers my tight hole.

"Play with your clit, baby," he murmurs, and I obey. My lower abdomen tightens and coils as I cry out in pleasure. I'm about to fall over the edge. Just at the precipice of desire, of my orgasm, when suddenly he stops.

He pulls his fingers from my body, and his tongue halts all movements.

"Stop touching yourself." His order is swift,

commanding, causing my hand to drop.

"What? Why?" I spin around, finding his feral stare burning a hole through me.

"We're going to play a little game." He smiles. He washes my front, then uses another body wash on himself, which reminds me of cinnamon and spice.

Once we're both clean, he shuts off the taps and steps from the shower. I watch as he wraps a towel around his waist, then calls me to join him. My nipples harden in the chilly room, but he moves quickly to dry my body from head to toe.

"Place your hands on the counter and bend over," he orders.

"Why?"

"Peyton, stop questioning me. Just do it." His words aren't harsh, but they leave no room for debate. Leaning over, I do as he says. He snaps the cap of a tube I notice is lube and drizzles enough over my ass to cause me to shiver. Then he picks up a silver butt plug with a pink diamond on the end and goes to work.

He's gentle, working the metal plug into my ass. Pain and pleasure intermingle, making me grip the counter, almost clawing at it. Once it's inside me, he rises and smirks at me in the mirror.

"You'll wear that all day. We'll head out for some lunch and shopping."

"You want me to go out with this thing in my ass?" I retort, spinning around. I feel full. Strange. But not bad at all. Carrick reaches around, swatting my ass which has a yelp falling from my lips.

"It will be your second test." He winks, stalking from the bathroom, leaving me gaping at his nonchalant smugness. Shaking my head, I follow him into the bedroom where he's laid out a beautiful sundress the color of pink cotton candy.

"Where's my underwear?" I question, lifting the dress and finding nothing else waiting for me.

"You won't wear any. Don't worry. I'll be the only one who knows you're naked underneath," he tells me as he's pulling on a crisp blue shirt. I can't drag my gaze away, watching him button it up. He's perfect in every sense of the word.

"I can't not wear panties, Carrick." I sound frustrated. I've never gone commando, as they say, and with this thing in my ass, it feels even more embarrassing.

"You can, and you will, Kitten. Now get dressed. We're going to be late." With that, he stalks from the bedroom, leaving me sighing once more. This man is insufferable. Frustrating. But I still can't help smiling at how easy it is to be with him.

When we stopped outside one of the boutique stores, I was too nervous to think about Carrick buying me anything. I've spent the past few years of my life working hard for my money, and frivolous shopping sprees were a thing of the past. But, he insisted, and now I'm standing in the dressing room with a beautiful, red, floor-length, silk dress.

The slit trailing its way up to my hip is kept together by red lace holding the cut down to my thigh, so if I do shift, or even turn too quickly, no one will get a glimpse of my pussy.

When I agreed to model the outfits for him, his eyes shimmered with a hungry fire that made me excited to do it, to allow him to command what I wear. It's a strange feeling. Each time he orders me to do something, I initially want to offer a snarky retort, but it's the affection he offers that makes me want to ensure I please him.

He looks at me like I'm a princess, and there's nothing that will deter me from giving him the pleasure he deserves. I want him to smile at me the way he did when he found me kneeling on the floor for him. As soon as I rose, I met those beautiful eyes that look right through the shyness I hide behind, and I knew, the grin he gifted me was one I wanted to see on his face forever.

"Are you okay in there, Kitten?" His voice comes from the other side of the door, startling me.

"Yes, give me a second," I call to him before taking one last glance in the mirror. My long blonde hair hangs in cascading waves down my back. The stiletto heels he chose to go with the dress give me a few extra inches, but even with them on, I'll still be shorter than Carrick.

Unlocking the door, I step out into the private fitting area. There are three sofas adorning the space with mirrors surrounding us. He's dressed in a light blue button up, with the cuffs rolled up to his elbows. A dark pair of slacks hug his muscled thighs and shiny black shoes adorn his feet. His hair is disheveled—sexy and messy. There's a light dusting of stubble on his angular jaw making him look elegantly rough. The man is a contradiction in every way.

I stand, awaiting his perusal of my body. He doesn't speak as his eyes sensually drag over me. He lifts a finger, twirling it around. I slowly take a turn, allowing him to see me from all angles.

"Fuck," he utters once I've completed a three-sixty. "You're exquisite. I'm tempted to rip that dress from your beautiful body right now."

My mouth curls into a teasing smirk I know will only land me in trouble, but I can't help enjoying the playfulness he's exuding. "Oh really, Sir?" I quip playfully, popping my hip before I tease. "And may I remind you, I'm not wearing any panties under the dress." My voice is a whisper, but I know he's heard me when his stare turns molten.

"Come here, Kitten," he bites out gruffly. I stroll over with confidence as his gaze simmers over my body. "Lift your dress, turn around, and bend at the waist," he says but doesn't make a move to rise or even touch me.

Easily, I lift the silk until it's bunched up over my naked ass. When I bend over, I'm open to him. The plug is still snugly in the tight hole of my ass. I'm about to ask him what to do when a resounding swat lands on the right cheek, then the left, and echoes around us. He continues to assault my now burning ass until I'm whimpering and wet. My core slick with need for him.

"Stand. I want you to change so we can purchase this dress and the shoes, then I'm taking you home."

He doesn't need to tell me what's going to happen when we get there. My mind can formulate my spanking was only the beginning.

Thirteen

Carrick

I've got a scene planned, but as soon as I pull up to the club, there's a cab leaving. Then I realize my brother and sister may have just arrived. Early, no less.

"You're about to meet the family, Kitten," I utter, exiting the car. When I round the front, I find Peyton has already gotten out. "In future, I open your door. Do you understand me?"

"Yes, Sir," she pipes up, saccharine sweet words that turn my blood to boil with desire. I can't walk in there with a hard-on. "You do realize I've been able to open car doors for a long while now." Her quip causes me to turn.

Regarding her through a narrowed gaze, I shake my head. My palm is itching to spank that sass from her pert ass, but I'll have to reign it in for later. "In the past, you weren't mine. Right now, you are, and I will care for you the way I want to. If you don't like it, you'll have to get over it," I inform her while grabbing the bags from the trunk.

We silently make our way toward the entrance. Confidence rolls off her in waves, and I find myself in awe of her. She's slight, a tiny pixie beside me. Her body has enough curve to be beautiful while arched, bound, and pleasured, and that's my plan. Tonight, I'll take her into my black room and bind her with the silk rope Mason brought in from Europe. I want to see how much she can take before she finally shatters from a non-sexual orgasm.

Unlocking the door, I allow her to enter first as I follow. Once it clicks shut behind us, I stalk behind her into the main area of the club to find Mason and my brother, Callan, and Cayleigh, my little sister, who's no longer little sitting at the bar.

"Brother," she squeals, bounding from the stool and into my arms. I didn't realize how much I missed my family until I find them right here. Her body is hugged by a black tank top and tight jeans that cause my anger to flare like a beacon in the dark.

"What the fuck are you wearing, Leigh?" I hiss in her ear.

"I'm twenty-seven. You can't tell me what to wear, Rick," she admonishes me as if I'm the one who's in trouble. I don't need my little sister dressing like this, especially when she's in this club. The men here will use her up, and that's something I will not stand for.

"Like fuck I can't, Leigh," I bite out when a hand tentatively touches my shoulder. My eyes fall to Peyton who's looking at me like I'm wrong. "She's my little sister," I inform her.

"She's old enough to know what she wants, Rick." The soft voice of Peyton calms me, but I still feel the anger surging through me.

"Hi, I'm Leigh." My sister holds out her hand to my . . . girlfriend? Submissive? Fuck, how do I introduce her.

"I'm Peyton. Your brother is showing me the ropes," she says, causing Mason to chuckle in the background. Callan rises, stalks toward Peyton, and pulls her hand up to his mouth.

"I'm the handsome brother." He winks salaciously,

and I find myself wanting to punch him for touching her. She's not mine. She's not wearing my collar. Merely a student. But even as I think it, I know I'm lying to myself.

"Okay you two." I shove my way through, shaking hands with Cal on the way toward the bar. "Where's D?" I ask Mason.

"He's headed out to grab the delivery. I figured I'd keep the O'Leary clan company until you two returned." My best friend winks, downing his shot of whiskey before saluting a goodbye to us all.

He's not one for crowds. He enjoys playing with Savvie and another girl, but if he's not on stage, he's a loner. Perhaps that's why we always got along so well. The man is a solid foundation to my fucked-up existence at times. There's something about him though, something he hides. It's nothing to do with the business, but I know emotionally he's closed himself off to marriage, and it intrigues me.

I've always been curious about people. Spending my time perceiving what I think others keep to themselves, I think that's what made me so good at what I did. When

I needed to infiltrate a group to retrieve information for Dad, I could do it without being noticed. I knew people. Read them.

With Peyton, I can't fucking get into her mind.

"So, Rick," Leigh says, dragging me from my memories. "Dad said to give you a hug from him. He's been busy with . . ." her words taper off as we all three glance at Peyton. She doesn't know who I really am, which makes me nervous. I should tell her. It's not fair that I'm lying to her when I want honesty from her.

"I'll take the shopping up to the apartment," she says, clearly feeling uncomfortable. She grabs the bags and heads to the stairs, but I can't let her leave like that. Rushing after her, I place a hand on her arm, stopping her in her tracks.

"I'm sorry. I just . . . I thought I had time to tell you more about me before they arrived," I tell her, imploring her with my gaze. It's not an excuse. It's the truth.

"It's okay, Carrick. No personal details, remember?" she says with a smile, but it's fake, plastered on to keep me calm. She tugs free of my hold, and I watch her ascend the stairs. I can't stop her, can't admonish her.

It's my rule. Stupidly, I thought I could be the one who's aloof, but Peyton seems to have it down to a T.

"I'm sorry, Rick," Leigh tells me when I turn back to the bar. Her big eyes are a deep hazel, shimmering with flecks of gold. "I didn't realize she didn't know, but then I—"

"It's fine. She's . . . I just haven't told her."

"Who is she, brother?" Callan questions, gulping his whiskey. His eyes are darker than both mine and Leigh's. They're a coffee color, and they seem to pierce me in that moment, digging into my mind to find out why there's a woman who looks so much like Aurora in my apartment and club.

"I'm training her."

"How exciting!" My sister bounces excitedly, but I don't hold the same enthusiasm. I can't. How can I when all I want is to feel something other than affection for Peyton? I wasn't meant to care for her, but I find myself wanting her more than I ever thought possible.

"Calm down, Leigh," I tell her, hoping she'll not get attached to Peyton the way she did with Rory. There was a sweetness in the relationship, sisters in arms. Each moment they spent together was just more time that my sister cried over. I don't need to see her agony again.

"Maybe she'll get that stick out from your ass." Callan chuckles, earning him a swat from our sister. "What? It's true. He needs to lighten the fuck up." One thing about my brother, he always says what's on his mind. There's never a time you'll wonder what he thinks of you.

"Are you two staying upstairs?" I question, glancing between them. When we're all three together, there's a camaraderie that warms my soul. I know I couldn't have survived losing the woman I love without them there. The support and affection they offered got me through the darkness that seemed to envelop me.

"Yeah. If you don't mind, of course. Now that you have a little toy to play with." Callan snorts. My gaze lands on him, pinning him with an angry glare. "What? I'm just joking. When does this place open? I need to find myself someone delicious to devour." His words incite worry in my mind. I know my brother isn't a Dominant as such, but he does love toys, and he enjoys women submitting, allowing him to do anything he wants to them.

"In an hour. Let's get you settled, and perhaps after, you can come down and watch Mason and Savvie's show," I offer, grabbing my sister's suitcase. Allowing them to follow me up the stairs, I take them through the hallway and into the elevator that takes us to the landing with two doors beckoning. One mine, one Mason's. However, there's a third floor I reserve for guests. We take the short flight of stairs to the apartment that we normally house any guests in.

It's beautifully furnished, but I never had an inkling to make it mine. Mason has always preferred the penthouse as well, even though this one has its own floor. However, most nights he spends at Savvie's place. I've always wondered how long he'll wait to propose or finally collar her. It's been years, but for some reason, the man is just enjoying what he has now.

"Wow, this place is amazing," Leigh murmurs behind me as I lead them into the wide-open space.

Modern furnishings greet us. With dark tiles and white walls, the area looks like it's straight from a magazine. "You're welcome to stay as long as you like," I inform them. "There's food in the fridge, four bedrooms, living room, kitchen, and each bedroom has an en suite."

"Thank you, big brother." Leigh swings her arms around my neck, holding me close until my eyes mist. I never cry. I didn't even cry when Rory was killed, but right now, having my little sister hang on me as if I'm her world, I allow the emotion to travel through me. Just for now.

"Thanks, Rick," Cal utters, patting me on the back. "I'll head to the shower. See you later," he says. My brows furrow in confusion. He's always been aloof, but he's even more so now than normal.

"Is he okay?" I question my sister, who nods. "He seems . . ."

"He's just feeling angry that he has to be here instead of London with the woman he's been shagging," she says, her British accent heavy on the final word. So, Callan's been fucking someone. My brother has always been a playboy, never caught up in one person, so this is news to me.

"And he's all caught up over one woman?" She shrugs in response. "Listen, I want you both to enjoy your time here. Hell, stay if you want to. But, I need to go and talk to Peyton." I pull Cayleigh into my arms, enveloping her in a hug so tight she's mumbling about losing all ability to breathe.

"I've missed you, Rick. It's not the same without you. Even Dad isn't the same without you." I nod, swallowing the emotional lump in my throat.

"I'll see you later, Leigh. Tell Cal to get that stick out from up his ass and join us downstairs in an hour." She giggles as I make my way out of the apartment and down to my own. Upon entering, I find a blonde beauty moving around the kitchen as if she owns it.

"Oh," Peyton squeals when I step into the space, startling her. "I thought you were spending the evening with your family, so I made some ravioli, but it's only one portion," she tells me, gesturing to the stove where two pots are boiling. Something in them smells delicious.

"We need to talk." My ominous words have her pretty brows scrunching in confusion. "It's about my family." Peyton nods, settling on the chair opposite me. The soft simmer of the water and sauce cooking behind us calms me, but what I'm about to tell Peyton is going to leave me raw.

I never thought I'd need to do this. To confess, admit who I really am. It's been so long since I've even accepted it, made mention of it. Everything feels foreign. As if I'm out of my depth.

"Look, Carrick, you really don't have to tell me anything if you don't want to," she says, sensing my fear in admitting it, in finally offering more of myself than I wanted to. "I understand you said no personal details, and this certainly seems personal."

I nod. "It is, but . . ." My words taper off into silence. Into the nothing that exists between us. That's where my problem lies. All the women I've been with before having been just that--nothing. They've meant nothing to me, until Peyton. And I can't explain why, but I want her to understand who I am. What I was. My name isn't just Carrick Anderson. She needs to know where my roots lie.

Fourteen

Peyton

He sits silently, and I want to hold him. I want to pull him into my arms and promise I'm not going anywhere, but what he's about to tell me clearly has him tense. His shoulders are bunched, the way his shirt tightens around his biceps tells me he's more than worried.

There's tension between us, swirling in the room. I hold my breath, wanting to hear every word, but my heart is pounding in my ears. If I told him how I felt, how I'm slowly falling for him and his brand of dominance, I'll either lose him, or I'll lose myself.

Gold eyes meet my green ones. They hold anguish so profound I feel it in my soul. He always does this to me. Makes me feel more than I should. We're meant to be nonexclusive. No strings. No emotion. But I can't help myself when he looks at me like that. As if I'm the only thing holding him together.

"Peyton, my real name is Carrick Aiden O'Leary." His words don't make sense. I've met him and learned his name. It's Carrick Anderson. "I'm . . . I've spent a few years in America after walking out on my family." Shaking my head, I reach for his hands, needing to touch him. To ground myself to him, and him to me. My heart leaps into my throat when he finally shakes his head and cups my cheeks.

There's pain dancing in those beautiful golden orbs, flickering like a flame about to engulf me in the inferno. "I don't understand," I hear myself say, but my voice is raspy. I feel like crying for him, because I have a feeling whatever is coming next will inadvertently break my heart.

"I left London because there was an accident. Eight years ago." He once again falls silent, and I realize what he's trying to tell me. It's why he's so closed off. So guarded. He lost someone he loves. His chest expands as he inhales a deep breath.

"It's okay, you don't have to—"

"I do." He places a finger on my lips to silence me.

"I was in church," he starts, causing my heart to ache, to squeeze so tight my chest feels as if it's caving in on me. I didn't realize how much I wanted him, how much I felt for him until he mentioned he had someone else. "I was waiting for my sister to get married."

"Okay," I respond, warily now because I'm not sure I want to hear this.

"There were so many gunshots. Too many to count. I fell on my sister, covering her, keeping her safe, but . . ." The lowering of his already gentle rumble causes me to lean forward. To swallow every word, to bask myself in his pain. Dropping my gaze to our hands, I notice how they're linked, fingers twining around each other. Needy. Wanting. "The woman I was engaged to was killed. Aurora. She…" Deep breath. "She was a beautiful blonde with piercing green eyes. There was a time I thought I couldn't love, and then she happened to me."

Why does it feel as if my lungs can't pull in air? Why do I feel like I'm drowning?

"My family is part of the Irish Mob, Peyton." It's then he meets my curious gaze. A gasp echoes around us, falling from my lips. Shaking my head, I release his hands. Tugging away as if I'm on fire, I rise too quickly, knocking the chair over. *Blonde, green eyes, Irish mob.* No. No!

I can't do this again. Michael was a henchman of the mafia in New York. He did things that would make horror movies seem like Disney. Shaking my head, I stumble backward, knocking a glass from the counter, and it shatters along with my heart.

"I . . ."

"Peyton," he says my name as a plea. I watch him rise. My feet don't allow me to move. They root me to the spot like concrete. His body is before me, looming, warm, but the danger I see in his eyes grip my throat. It tightens its hold on me. "I'll give you space. I know this is a lot to take in."

"I need to go home." I find my voice. It's husky, filled with shock. "I . . . I can't be here." Before he can come any closer, I'm racing through the living room, pulling on a sweater. My bones feel as if the cold has seeped into them.

"Peyton, please?" He's begging. I'm breaking him as much I'm broken. I'm shattering everything I've wanted. Carrick made me feel, he gave me something to ache for, to indulge in, but this is done. I can't go through sleepless nights again.

"Carrick, this was . . . We were never meant to be here." I don't know what I mean, his brows furrow in confusion, and I know I'm not making any sense. My brain feels as if it's spinning out of control. *Irish mob, blonde, green eyes.*

The words replay in my mind like a broken record. Looping. Again and again.

"I'm not a consolation prize, Carrick." I spin on my heel, shocking him at the ferocity of my words. "What did you do? Picture her while fucking me? Did you want to call out her name while my pussy was squeezing your cock?" With each question, I punch him in the chest. Not that he feels it. He doesn't even flinch.

"Listen to me," he starts, but I continue.

"No. You listen to me. I'm not a slave you can use for your own sick pleasure. Was I her replacement? Is that why you wanted me so much?"

"No!"

His response booms around me, knocking the fight

from me. I blink. Tears stream down my face, but I don't wipe them away. I don't want to. I need him to see what he did to me.

"Is this what control you'd like to have over me? Make me feel something, and then tell me how I'm the ghost you've been fucking for the past few days?"

"No. You're not her. You're not a ghost either. That's why I told you, I—"

"Do you have a photo of her?" The question stills him for a moment. He doesn't move, a solid statue of agony. He nods. "Let me see. I need to see her," I tell him adamantly. He reaches for his wallet, pulls out a small square photo of him and a woman who could've been my twin. She was beautiful.

The photo blurs when more salty emotion spills from my eyes. He wanted me only to have her back in his life. He didn't really want me. He made it clear.

"This wasn't how I foresaw things to go. I didn't think I'd ever love again." His confession knocks the air from my lungs. Snapping my gaze to him, I drop the photo on the table, not caring if it falls to the floor, but he doesn't move.

"Love?" I cough out the word on a chuckle. "You know nothing about the word love, Carrick Anderson, O'Leary, whatever the fuck your name is. I came here, agreed to be yours to learn, but I didn't agree to be a stand in for the woman you lost."

I pivot, heading for the door, but before I can even wrench it open, his body is there, against my back. His hand on the wall, caging me in, the other holding my exit shut. I can't move. He's too strong, and I've lost my fight.

"Don't go." His words drip with such anguish, I turn to face him, to look into his eyes. I want to believe it's me he wants, but how can I?

"Why?" He doesn't respond immediately, and I have a feeling he's trying to choose his words very carefully. His eyes burn into me, setting me on fire. This is the seduction of Carrick. He's beautiful, he's broken, and my soul cries out because I want him to be mine. But he's not. He can't be if he's holding on to a faded memory. Holding on to a woman who's gone.

"I need you, Peyton," he offers then. We stare at each other for a long moment, heavy with emotion, with the fragility of what we have. I knew I'd succumb to his ministrations. I've fallen, head first, and I didn't even plan on it. Nothing about Carrick is safe. There's a danger about him, but it's not because of his family ties or what he's done in his past. No, it lurks beneath the surface of his chest, that cracked heart that holds love for *her,* and the emotion he's so desperately trying to grasp for me.

"You need me?"

"Yes," he hisses, leaning in, inhaling my scent. He's as addicted to me as I am to him.

"Do I smell like her?" I don't know why I ask, but I do. The words fall from my mouth unbidden, but they're there, hanging between us like a lead weight.

"No. Nothing about you is like her. You're pure, beautiful, and there's an innocence to you that I want to mark, I want to claim."

"Wasn't she innocent?" My throat closes when he snaps his gaze to mine. The fire that rages through him singes me, slow and deliberate. He's doing it on purpose, showing me inside his heart, his mind.

"She was the daughter of one of my father's

associates. A mob boss's daughter. She was far from innocent. We found each other in darkness, and I knew that's where we'd stay until the day a bullet took one of us out. But I didn't realize the moment for her would come so soon."

He releases me then. Stepping back, he waits for me to run, but I don't. If there's one thing my mother taught me, it was to stand my ground. Fight for what I want. Never give up. But to fight for a man who loves another, that's something else entirely. I want Carrick, but he lied. At least, he didn't admit that I looked like his ex and that was the only reason he wanted me. I was a ghost he was holding onto, and that slices me deeper than anything else.

"She gave me purpose for the time she was in my life, but you . . ." His words taper into nothing, into the air around us that sizzles. Suddenly, there's a loud screeching beep, and I realize the pots must've set off the alarm. Carrick races into the kitchen, shoving open the windows, turning off the cooker.

"Shit," I utter when I see the dark smoke against the pristine white walls. Tears burn my eyes in that moment.

Like my love for Rick, which is going up in smoke, so I've ruined his home. I should leave. I shouldn't be here. My heart aches at the thought of walking away.

"It's fine." He doesn't look at me. His gaze is trained on the open window. His hands grip the sink in a white-knuckle grip. "Peyton, you stumbled into my life, and I didn't think I could love you. I agreed to train you because you looked like her, but I chose you because I hated her for leaving me, even though it wasn't her choice. I hated how life stole her from me, and I was convinced I could never love again, even If the girl looked like her. But it happened. I want you, Peyton."

"Rick, I can't do this." He pivots, his eyes on mine in an instant, stealing my breath just like he always does. "I . . . I mean, I understand how you can love someone so much you need them in your life. But, this is so much more. I can't be second best, or a consolation prize."

I don't know how to take his explanation. Part of my heart wants to go to him. The other half wants to walk out the door. But how can I when I've fallen, when my soul sings for him? My body craves him, aches for his touch. My mouth hungers for his kiss.

"You're not a fucking consolation prize." His anger vibrates through him. It hurts me. It shatters him, and I realize I've done this as much as he has. We've broken each other. This is not right. When you love someone, you're meant to heal them, to put them back together, not completely obliterate them.

Perhaps it's stupid. Maybe it's because I begged him to take my innocence. To violate the promise I gave Michael because he hurt me, and I could no longer hold onto the girl I was with him. She was gone, and in her place was a woman.

But when he turns to regard me once more, I know none of that is true. I see it shining clearly in his eyes. I'm in love with Carrick, and he's in love with me. He doesn't say it. He implores me with his gaze to understand. It's shining in the gold flecks. His hands fist at his sides, and I know he's holding onto his restraint. Shaking my head, I step back. He doesn't follow, and I don't expect him to.

The man can be loving and caring, but he can also be cold and controlled. A commanding force when he needs to be, and now I know the truth as to why he is like that. A soldier. Taught and trained to kill.

"Peyton, there's nothing more I can say. But what I need you to know is that it's you. You're the one who changed me. In a short time, you are the one who's given me more than I can imagine having in my life. I'm no good for you, but I'll never stop trying to win your heart."

"I thought we weren't putting our hearts out there?" I'm sassing him, questioning him when all he needs is understanding. But right now, I can't give him that.

"The rules are broken. They broke the moment I realized I wanted you. Not her, not any other woman in this place. You." His words are raw with honesty. They steal my breath the same way he stole it the moment he kissed me that first night.

"The rules were in place to keep us safe," I tell him.

"Fuck the rules, Peyton. I haven't been safe since you stumbled into my life," Carrick growls. "And I don't regret a thing." His body vibrates from the opposite side of the kitchen island. My gaze roves over him once more before I nod.

"I need time," I tell him. It's all I can give him right now. Perhaps time to re-evaluate my life, my heart, my emotions. Learning the man you love was with you because you remind him of his dead ex is not something that can easily be overcome.

"Okay."

I turn, grabbing my purse, and head for the door. My hand trembles when I reach for the handle and twist it. I'm on the threshold when he calls out to me. It's so quiet I almost don't hear it.

"I'll be here when you come back."

Not if, but when.

I don't respond.

My heart doesn't allow me to.

FIFTEEN

CARRICK

The door clicked shut, and my world shattered around me. I didn't want this to happen. It wasn't meant to go like this, but like I learned early on in life, you can't control someone else's love. You can't beg them or force them to love you.

Even though I know she does, I close my eyes and let the sadness drain from me. I meant what I said to her. I'll never stop fighting for her heart. She's mine. She will always be mine, even if we're not together. There's so much more to what we found with each other.

Yes, we probably fucked up more than we would ever care to admit, but when she walked out, she broke me. The man who always held onto all the control finally lost it. And it left with a pretty little blonde girl who's stolen everything from me.

Perhaps she knows I'm not good enough for her. A killer. Why would she want someone like that in her life? She needs someone good. Who can love her and give her a family. Not a man who has been trained to kill.

Anger races through me. I can't stop swiping my hand over the counter sending the glasses and bottle of wine shattering to the ground. Glass flies in every direction, splintering like the way her eyes did when I confessed my sins to her.

Of course she walked out. I can't blame her. The anger I'm feeling is not for the girl I want, but toward myself. I fucked up. As always. When I walked into the contract with her, I knew what I was getting myself into. It was done and dusted. I would train her. She'd walk away. However, nothing in my life is simple. I fell. And I fucking did it harder than I ever expected to.

Fuck this.

Stalking into the bedroom, I tug off the jacket I'm still wearing. Once I've shrugged my shirt off, I head into the bathroom and turn on the shower. Tonight, I'll lose myself in my work. Which means I'll take a woman who wants it hard and ensure she screams.

The water steams the small tiled space, and I step under the scalding water. Dropping my head back, I close my eyes and imagine her. Peyton Moore fucked with my heart. She unlocked it from the cage and held it in her hands with such fragility and innocence I couldn't stop my feelings for her.

Her body beneath mine, the plump lips she wrapped around my shaft, the way her whimpers echoed in my ears as I made her come haunt me. I scrub my skin. It's raw and red by the time I realize the spray is ice cold, but I revel in the ache. It's the only thing that makes me feel when the only person that made me feel alive walked out the door.

Stepping from the shower, I wrap a towel around my waist.

"Rick." Cal's voice comes from the doorway. I turn to find my brother glaring at me from the threshold. His arms folded across his chest, the black dress shirt he's wearing looks as if it's about to rip with his muscles bulging in the material.

"What?" My answer is spit in frustration as I disappear into my closet. Pulling out charcoal slacks and a silver button-up, I find him sitting in the chair at the window where I once sat and watched Peyton sleep in my bed. Under my fucking sheets.

"Jesus, you look like someone pissed in your cornflakes." He chuckles. "Did the pretty blonde who raced out of here in tears have something to do with that look in your face?" He's a smart ass, and I feel like kicking him out of my apartment, but I don't. This is how we are. He pisses me off, and I tell him to go fuck himself.

"Fuck you, Callan," I grunt out, shrugging on the fresh shirt. He watches me button it up. His one foot over the opposite knee. Pulling out a cigarette, I glare at him as he lights it in my bedroom. "Can you not do that in here?"

"What happened to you, brother?" His question jars me, angers me.

"What happened to me?" I respond incredulously. Stalking toward him, I lean in. Ripping the smoke from his fingers, I place it between my lips and pull the nicotine into my lungs. The hit is hard, knocking the breath from me. It's been years since I had a smoke. Years since I did anything other than lose myself in a drink. "I lost my fucking fiancée," I grit out through clenched teeth.

He cocks his head to the side. Curiosity burning in his dark eyes. "Really? You're still hung up over Rory? Or is this new stick up your ass got something to do with the little blonde doll who ran out of here crying her heart out?"

Shoving away from him, I saunter into the bathroom to finish getting dressed. Once I'm clothed, I ignore Callan and make my way into the living room with him hot on my heels.

"Tell me, Rick, is there a reason why you chose a woman who looks like your dead ex-fiancée?"

"I didn't do it on purpose. Hell, I figured if I could fuck her and move on, I'd be fine," I tell him, pouring us both a double shot of Jameson Irish whiskey. Placing his tumbler on the counter, I down mine in one gulp and pour another shot.

"And you're not fine," he says, the English lilt of his voice carrying through. He finishes the shot, sliding the glass along the mahogany top toward me. Once the glass has another three fingers in it, he takes it and downs it in one swallow. The wince on his face makes me chuckle.

"Seems you're not fine either," I respond. He doesn't answer. Instead, he flops on my sofa. The apartment door flies open, and there, in a beautiful silk dress, is my little sister. Jesus, I need to stop calling her that. She's about to turn twenty-eight, but to me, she's still the baby of the three of us. Callan being thirty-seven, and me being thirty-six.

"Are you two going to sit up here all night, wallowing in self-pity?" she questions. Her hands on her hips like my mom used to do. She was a feisty woman. She scared all of us when she took on that stance. We knew we'd be whipped with the belt when we'd done something naughty.

"Have a drink with us, Leigh," Cal says. Crooking his finger, he calls her over.

I grab another glass and pour a shot, knowing my sister is much more tomboy than homecoming queen. She used to drink whiskey with us boys when she turned sixteen. It was the only way we got through knowing what we were in for as we got older.

I pour three drinks. Lifting my glass in the air, I

utter, "To the O'Leary siblings."

"Family first and forever," we all respond in unison. The family motto still rings true. With the three of us together again, my heart swells with pride, but my mind is awash with guilt. I walked out on them when they needed me most. Cayleigh most of all.

"Where's your girl?" she questions, causing my body to turn rigid. "Oh, Jaysus, Carrick." Her Irish accent, strong when she curses, echoes through me. "What'd you do to the girl?"

"Nothing, Leigh. Just drink your whiskey, and let's get downstairs. I have work to do." I shouldn't take that tone with her, but I can't talk about Peyton right now. I can't think about her, but that doesn't stop my mind wandering to where she is, what she's doing.

"You can't keep running, big brother," Leigh admonishes me. I know why she says that, because it's what I do, but this time, it wasn't me who ran. I stayed, I gave her the honesty, and she said she needed time. Needed to think things through. As much as I want to be angry at her, I'm not. I should've given her honesty right from the start. That's what I asked for, but I couldn't bring myself to voice the words.

We walk down the steps into the club that's slowly filling with men and women dressed in formal attire. The evening is meant to be elegant yet relaxed. But most of the Dominants here are in three-piece suits. I don't go that far. I never do. A suit and tie are my norm. Other than that, I'll be in jeans and a button-up.

"Well, who's that?" Leigh questions, leaning into my shoulder. I follow her gaze to find one of my longest serving clients and best friends, Oliver Michaelson. Dressed in a silver suit, black dress shirt, and a white tie, he looks ever the Dominant with his rigid form.

"No." I utter one word. Leaving her to gawk from a distance, I saunter away with only that answer for my little sister who I will not allow to be taken on by Oliver. I trust him with my life. But he's a sadist. And my sister will not be getting whipped and spanked by him, or any other man in this room.

Cayleigh's small clicking footsteps are hot on my heels as I make my way to the bar. "What? Why? What's wrong with him?" she squeaks. Yes, she really fucking squeaks at me. "Rick, answer me?"

"You're not to go into any of those back rooms. Do you understand me, Leigh?" My order only causes her face to heat bright red. She was planning it. The wheels in her pretty little head are already turning. I know her better than I know myself, and she's definitely one to defy the rules, which only makes me sigh.

"You can't tell me what to do, Rick. This is my life and my choice." Her words are true. It is her life, but she's my blood.

"You're old enough to know better," I tell her, lifting three fingers at Dylan. He nods and starts pouring my drink. I want a whiskey tonight, but I don't keep Jameson down here, so the gin will have to do.

"I do know better. Why is it you're able to do as you please, but I can't? I'm not your little sister anymore, Rick," she admonishes me, the same way my mother would. A thought slams into me then. She'll be a wonderful mother. And if that godforsaken shooting had never happened, she may have been. Her fiancé was killed in cold blood, and her dress bore the stains.

"You cannot go with Oliver." My voice is adamant.

"Why is that, Rick?" The smooth baritone of Mr.

Michaelson sounds behind me. My sister blushes at his presence, and I can only groan in resignation. As much as I want my sister safe, I know he's the only one in this club who will ensure she is. He's experienced, he trains submissives all the time, but what man wants to know his sister is about to get flogged, bound, and tortured?

"Oli," I respond, reaching out a hand he accepts and shakes. His amused smile does nothing to quell the frustration at Leigh's insistence. "I was just telling my *little* sister"—I emphasis little as if it would make a difference, which I know it won't— "she's still new to all this."

"Well," he starts, taking her hand, pressing a kiss to her knuckles in a show of chivalry. "I'll take good care of her," he tells me but doesn't avert his gaze from Leigh. She's smitten. Her cheeks are bright red as she smiles up at the man.

"I'm Cayleigh," she tells him, her voice sugary sweet.

"What a beautiful accent," he coos, and I feel the need for much more alcohol than I planned on drinking tonight. Oliver glances up at me. He's asking permission.

My sister's gaze burns into me. If there's one thing I can't do, it's refuse her.

I nod, and that's Oli's cue to lead her off to the back rooms. I don't know which one he's chosen, and frankly, I don't want to know. Turning back to the bar, I grab both her abandoned glass and mine and down both shots.

"Are you on a bender?" Callan sidles up beside me, settling onto the bar stool. He grabs a drink and swirls it in his hand.

"I'm just trying to get the image of Leigh getting spanked by a much older Dominant out of my head," I tell him. He chuckles, lifting the glass to his lips. I signal Dylan for another round as I finally take a seat.

The lights dim, and I know Mason and Savvie are up on stage soon. When the announcer steps up to the mic, I can't help but smile. Eva looks incredible. She was my project when I found her at sixteen on the streets. She thinks I gave her a full submissive experience then, but she had no idea how easy I went on her.

There was an elegance about her. Even in the tattered clothes, she exuded beauty. She's exquisite, and I can see why Nathan is so enamored with her. Since he's claimed her, they moved to the West Coast, opening a branch of Sins in the city. I didn't realize they were here.

She announces the act and steps off stage. I watch in awe as the Merlot-colored fabric hugs her curves as she heads straight for me. Before she reaches Callan and me, Nate is at her side as I expect him to be.

"Darling." I lean in, pressing a kiss to each of her cheeks. "You look exquisite," I offer, roving my gaze up and down her form.

"She does, doesn't she?" Nate shakes my hand. "We're expecting," he tells me proudly, and that's when I notice the tiny bump of her stomach. She's positively glowing, and that's why.

"Congratulations. You're both going to be incredible parents," I tell them, offering each of my friends a hug. We're very close; they're like family. "This is my brother, Callan," I introduce Cal, who offers them a smirk.

"Good to see my little bro has some friends around him." He chuckles, shaking Nathan's hand. When he glances at Eva, I can tell he's smitten by her.

"We'll always be there for Rick. If it wasn't for him, we wouldn't be married," Nathan says with a smile that lights up the room. "We'll see you later," Nate tells me, moving over to order drinks for them both.

Once we're alone, I can't help noticing my brother's attention on a table in the far corner.

"You okay, Cal?"

He snaps his gaze to me, then back to the table. "Who's the stunner with the red dress?" he questions, taking a drink of the beer he ordered moments ago. I stare at the girl for a moment, trying to place her. She's familiar, but I can't think of where I've seen her before.

It's only when she laughs, rises, then heads toward the bar that I see her face properly. "No, Callan. Do not even touch that," I warn. "That's the senator's daughter."

He shrugs, and I realize I've just fucked up. When you tell Callan not to do something, he does it because he wants to piss you off. I guess the O'Leary kids do have something in common after all.

"Why?" he questions, not casting his glance to me.

"She's sweet, innocent, and she's not to be mauled by an animal like you," I hiss in his ear, earning myself a guffaw. "Trust me, Cal. That's a family you do not want to piss off."

"Who said I wanted the family? Perhaps I just want the sweet little cunt that's under that red silk," he confirms, pushing off the stool, leaving me staring after him.

SIXTEEN

PEYTON

Savannah is perched on the bed watching me intently. Her blue eyes probe me for answers I can't give. For some reason, I haven't been able to admit that Carrick and I are over. I didn't want it to be, but I needed time to think things through.

When Carrick confessed about his past, I knew I needed time to figure this out. I've been in a relationship with a man who had ties to the mafia, and it's part of the reason I don't know if I can do it again. Michael was dangerous; at least I learned that before I walked down the aisle. I know Carrick has moved on from that life, but how easy would it be for him to fall back into it?

"Peyton, I'm not stupid. And neither is Mason." Hearing her Dominant's name causes me to turn around and finally face my best friend. "He told me Rick is in bad shape." Her words slice me wide open. I still love him. I think I always will. He opened my mind to more, my body and heart to things I never thought I'd be able to accept.

It's who I am now.

"I can't be with him, Savvie," I tell her, pulling the sleek black dress up my body until it's fitted around me like a glove. I'm about to speak when a knock at the door sounds, making my heart flutter wildly in my chest.

"I'll get it." Savvie pushes up from the bed, heading for the door. "If it's Rick, I'm telling him you ran off with some rich man to get married."

"No!"

Her laugh echoes through the space. She knows me better than anyone else, and there's no way I can hide my feelings for Carrick from her. I've tried over the years to keep myself guarded, and she's the only one who's ever seen through my bullshit. Well, apart from Chance.

"Pey." My brother's voice trails through the hallway, and then he's at the entrance to my bedroom. Dressed in a pair of dark jeans, a white button-up, and his fancy dress shoes, he looks like a model just off the runway.

"You're here," I gasp, racing to him, pulling him into a hug, inhaling his spicy cologne. "I've missed you." My words are muffled in his shirt, but he hears me.

"Savvie said you needed some girl time, so here I am," he utters with a flourish that has me giggling. It feels good to laugh. His arms are strong around my small frame, making me wish he could keep me safe from all the pain in my heart. I've had a broken heart before, but this is different.

I recall reading a quote online about the love a submissive gives, and it is different to how I loved Michael. I think when you offer someone control over every part of you, there's a trust that burrows itself deep, right down to your soul.

And that's how I love Rick.

"I just needed time to recover from the past few days," I tell my brother. Once again, he sees through my lies and shakes his head.

"Please. You and this man who's got you all wound up is the reason I'm here." Savannah joins us then, regarding me with a smile that is as mischievous as my brother's.

My gaze flits between the two of them, trying to figure out what they have up their sleeves. "What are you two planning?" I question, suddenly wary of the two people I care for most in my life. When they come together, there's never a dull moment. But this has something to do with Carrick, and right now, all I want to do is forget about him.

"We're heading to Sins," Savvie informs me easily. "There's someone I want you to meet."

"I can't go in there."

"Yes, you can," Chance tells me. "And I'm going with. We're going to meet a man named Oliver, and from what Savvie told me, he sounds utterly delicious." My brother already seems smitten, and he hasn't even seen this man before.

"And why am I meeting Oliver?" I question Savannah, my eyes narrowed on her in curiosity.

She lifts her hand, blowing on the wet nails she's been painting a bright purple. The color suits her pale skin and white-blonde hair. It's unnaturally light, but it definitely makes her unique in every way.

Her big sapphire eyes meet mine, her lips curling

into a playful grin. "Carrick will be jealous," she says nonchalantly. "Then, he'll make sure he claims you."

"Savvie, I don't want him to claim me."

"And I don't want Mason to marry me," she retorts with a sad smile. I know she loves that man more than anything, and the fact that he's still not proposed must break her heart. Perhaps he just doesn't want to get married. The whole institution of it is old school.

Sighing, I glance at my brother, who's smirking like a Cheshire cat. "And you're in on this, aren't you?" He nods, proud of the fact that he's just blindsided his sister. "You're both being ridiculous. I don't want to make Carrick jealous. It's best for us both if he moves on, and I will too."

"Exactly," Savannah confirms. "And when he sees you've moved on, he'll wake up and realize that you two were meant to be together,"

"But—" I say, trying to stall her tirade, but she ignores me, continuing with her explanation.

"But you'll see that you're not meant to move on. I've seen you and Carrick together. There's something there that you don't find every day."

"Savvie, he told me I look like his dead fiancée." I implore her to understand why it's so difficult for me to even consider being with him. "How do I know he's not fucking her while he's with me?"

She considers my question for a moment before she responds. "Because Carrick may be an asshole, but this is not something he can hide from either Mason or me. If my man says Rick is in love with you, I believe him."

Her words settle on my heart, calming my erratic heartbeat. Can I give him a chance? Will he be able to put his ex behind him and really be with me?

"Fine. But when this blows up, then it's on you," I tell her. "And you," I admonish Chance.

"Hey, I just want to see my sister happy." My brother hugs me. His body is warm, safe, and I just for a moment allow myself to believe everything will be okay. Nothing is ever confirmed. There are times I have doubted myself, until Carrick, but I can't let him be the deciding factor in my happiness. I need to move on.

"Are we ready?" Savvie says, rising from the bed with her purple dress matching her nails.

"As ready as I'll ever be."

"I've been ready for far too long," Chance utters with a naughty smile on his face, and I know he's going to be in his element with all the handsome men who frequent Sins.

We head to the door, and for the first time in days, I smile as I lock up the apartment and follow my brother and my best friend. Tonight, I may not be with anyone, but I'll allow myself to have some fun.

Stepping into Seven Sins has my heart racing a million miles a minute. I don't see him, but it doesn't stop my eyes from seeking him out. Wanting to find those golden eyes. Needing to see his handsome face, that smirk that melts my panties, and the voice that seems to light every nerve in my body.

"Oli," Savannah purrs when she reaches an older man seated at the bar. He's probably in his mid-forties from the light gray that peppers his black hair. His eyes are the color of steel, a shiny gray that looks right through me when his gaze lands on me.

"Savvie." He smiles, knocking the breath from

my lungs. Yes, he's handsome. He looks like he's been carved from marble. Perfect angular jaw, sharp features. Dressed in a suit that's a deep blue; so dark it's almost black, but when the light hits it the right way, I notice the tinge of blue. He pulls Savannah into a hug, planting a kiss on her cheek.

"And who are your beautiful friends?" he questions, flitting his eyes between Chance and me. There's a curiosity in his expression as he regards us both.

"This is my best friend, Peyton," she gushes as she pulls me closer. I feel out of my depth for the first time in a long while. Carrick always made me feel so comfortable, whereas Oliver seems to be too experienced to even give me a second glance. And as I think that, he leans in and brushes his lips over my cheek.

"Hello, sweet Kitten," he utters my nickname. I gasp as he steps back. "I know of you," he tells me, and I realize Carrick must have spoken to him already. But why? "And this?" Oliver's stare lands on Chance.

"This is Peyton's brother, Chance Moore."

My brother holds out his hand, but Oliver doesn't take it. Instead, he tips his head to the side, watching

Chance with a curious stare. I'm about to say something when he grips the back of my brother's neck, pulling him closer. The show of dominance has a few of the people surrounding us watching in awe.

His mouth lingers inches from Chance's, and I'm sure my brother is going to pass out from the shock of it all. Oliver's tongue flicks out, trailing over Chance's lips. "He's delicious," Oliver utters with a smirk. "Do you play?" he asks.

"No, I've never—"

"Perfect. I do love to train," the older man confirms with a satisfied smile. "If you'd be up for a scene, I'd love to have you along with someone else I've picked for the evening to join me."

"Yes. Yes, I'd love to." I gape at my brother's eagerness.

"It's settled. Peyton and I will watch a show while you two get acquainted." Savvie grips my arm, but Oliver stops her.

"No, I want Peyton in the toy room. Now." There's no denying this man. He pierces me with a confident stare. "Unless she's scared?" He's trying to goad me. I'm not scared. Far from it. His display has only solidified that I want to see what he's capable of.

A giggle from the corner booth distracts me for a moment. My eyes find Rick. He's sitting with another man. They're deep in conversation, but it's not the way he's laughing that makes me decide to go with Oliver. It's the woman perched on his lap. He's not touching her. But she's practically one with him the way she's draped herself over him.

His golden eyes land on mine in an instant. As if he can feel me. We're no longer together. We broke up, but it still stings. He smiles. Then turns back to his conversation.

"I'm not scared. Let's go," I finally confirm, hooking my arm through Oliver's. As we walk toward the back of the club, I feel him looking. His gaze always burned through me, and this time it's no different. This time, he's practically setting me alight with fury, and I smile as I'm led away by Oliver.

When we reach the room, the door is open, and Oliver allows me to step inside first. He follows, shutting the door behind us. The room is decked in black leather furniture, a spanking bench, and a four-poster bed. One wall is covered in toys that make fear trickle through me.

"What are you doing here?" he questions once we're alone.

I frown, meeting his inquisitive gaze. "What do you mean?" He settles on the sofa, watching me intently before he pats his knee. I take that as a silent command to sit on his lap. I take a step toward him, and he shakes his head.

"Crawl." My mouth drops open in shock. "Now." Dropping to my knees, I feel the cool concrete floor bite into my flesh. I crawl like a kitten on all fours to Oliver. "Head here," he tells me, and I obey, placing my hand on his knee, almost curling up between his legs like a pet would do.

He falls silent, his hand stroking my sleek blonde hair. It's gentle, sweet, and loving. I want to ask him what he's doing, but I hold my tongue. If he doesn't allow me to speak, I know to keep my mouth shut.

"Tell me, Peyton," he starts. "You came here tonight to play with someone?"

"Yes, Oliver," I respond.

He hums his approval, gripping the hair at the nape of my neck, he pulls me up until I'm inches from his face. He trails his nose up my neck slowly. He's not touched me in any sexual way, but my body has already been lit from the inside out.

"You like the darker side of this, don't you? You're a little masochist. Oh, I would have such fun with you. Too bad you're already claimed." He releases me, causing me to fall to the floor.

"What? I'm not claimed," I retort hotly, which causes him to chuckle.

"Feisty too. No wonder he's so enamored," he tells me, and I realize he's talking about Carrick.

Sitting up, I fold my arms in front of my chest. My eyes pin him with a confused stare. Anger races through my blood at the mention of Carrick laying any claim to me. "I'm not his. We are not together."

"Sweetheart, he's laid his claim. Any man in this club would be stupid to touch you."

"You brought me in here," I tell him. Confused at what he means. How can Carrick lay claim to me when I'm not with him anymore?

"I did. But I'm not afraid of Carrick O'Leary," he tells me, using Carrick's real name. "I know everything there is to know about any Dominant in this city. Most of them I've trained. I've even set them up with their submissives."

"Like Mason?"

"Mason, Nathan, who I don't think you've met, and of course there's Elijah." The last two men I don't know, but this intrigues me.

"So, you train subs and Dominants?"

"I do. There's a satisfaction in it for me. I love seeing someone come into their own. Find their sexuality. For a long time, Rick was like me. He took girls in, showed them there's more to life than being abused. Eva, one of his dear friends, as well as a pretty little sub called Gia. Both those girls are now with Rick's friends."

"With his friends? How can they do that?" I'm confused. More so than I was days ago. Nothing makes sense. The Carrick he's talking about sounds like a stranger to me.

"You see, Carrick loves to save those in need. Eva was his first. She loved him too much. She's with Nate now. And Gia, she was one of the girls who stumbled upon the club. And she found her Dominant, who's Elijah."

"And Rick helped them?" He nods.

"I wanted to bring you in here to tell you he's not a bad man. He may have done bad things, but . . ." His words trail off, and he rises. "You're beautiful. Stand," he commands. I obey.

"Thank you," I say. I'm not sure why I'm thanking him, but I do.

"Look after yourself. I really would've loved to play with you, but I have two eager toys waiting for me." He smiles. It's breathtaking.

"Are you going to . . .? I mean, my brother—"

"He's safe. He and the pretty little sub, Leigh, will be mine to play with."

"Cayleigh? Rick's sister?" I gasp in shock. Oliver nods a confirmation. "And he is allowing you to be with his sister?"

"You're a sweet girl. Rick doesn't *allow* anything. She came to me. I train those who want it. I don't take what isn't mine." He leans in, lingering against my ear before continuing, "Even though I'd so much want to see your porcelain skin bleed as I whip you."

My mind is reeling at his words. "What?"

"I'm a sadist. I enjoy delivering pain."

"Don't hurt—" He places his fingers on my lips to silence me.

"Go now. Before I can't help fucking your pretty little throat." He releases me, walks me to the door. "Take care of yourself, Peyton." Then the door shuts behind me, leaving me in the dimly light hallway. Before I have time to think, I'm being dragged into another room and shoved inside.

"What the fuck do you think you're doing?" Carrick bites out through clenched teeth. His jaw ticks with fury, and I can't help flinching at his words. He sounds livid. Pure rage vibrates through his body, causing me to shut my mouth. This isn't how this night was meant to go. He wasn't meant to be angry at me. As soon as I walked in and saw him with another woman, I figured we'd moved on.

"You have no right to be angry, Rick," I retort. "He . . . I mean, this is ridiculous. Oliver was lovely, caring, and I enjoyed the scene," I lie. There was no scene, but he doesn't need to know that. "You pushed me away by having some other little slut on your lap, Carrick." The crack in my voice breaks. It scratches along my throat like a raw wound, and I know nothing else can mend it but Carrick.

As I stalk toward him, I meet his gaze, which burns into me, setting me ablaze. This man has such power over me, but I have some over him too. I see it in his expression. As much as I want to deny it, I can't because I love him. My heart breaks, but I can't be with him after he's fucked someone else.

"You made me feel . . ." My words trickle into nothing. The emptiness where my heart had been ripped so violently from me is now filled with one man. With the one before me who's pushed me away. In the years I spent with Michael, I never ached. I never felt like the air was too thick to breathe. And I never saw a forever.

"You weren't meant to love me, Peyton," Carrick says. The pained emotion that flickers in his golden eyes makes me want to crawl to him. To give him all of me. Because as much as I guarded myself from him, nothing can dissipate my feelings.

"There are times you can't rule your heart, Sir." The affection he holds so close to his chest dances in his eyes at my words. "When you finally let go of the past and allow the happiness you're meant to have into your life, give me a call. But Carrick"—I lean up, pressing a kiss to his stubble cheek—"don't for one second believe I had a choice in loving you, because you made it impossible not to."

I turn and head toward the door of the room he's shoved me into and twist the doorknob. The sound seems to echo around me. It's deafening in the silence. When it shuts behind me, I blink, allowing the tears to fall.

I wanted him to follow me. To stop me from leaving, but he doesn't. My heart breaks all over again. How many times am I going to allow him to do this to me? I can't. Inhaling a deep breath, I escape the club and go home. I need time.

Seventeen

Carrick

Peyton walked out three days ago. Nothing prepared me for it. It's for the best. She shouldn't be near me. I'll only hurt her. My life was meant to be lived alone. I learned that from a very early age. My father never lied to me. He never gave me empty promises and told me one day I'd be able to have a family.

Even after walking out and leaving my family behind, I can never leave this life. I know that now. My office door swings open, and Callan saunters in with a grin on his face.

"What?" I question, sitting back in my office chair.

"There's a redhead downstairs I've been chatting up," he tells me. He's a flirt. My brother is worse than me. His dick is perpetually wet.

"I didn't allow you into my club to fuck everything

with tits, Cal," I huff, shoving the paperwork over the desk toward him.

He chuckles as he lifts the folder from the wooden top. "Not my fault my brother has so many delicious little cunts walking around."

"Jesus, would you have some respect, man?" I bite out. Rising from the chair, I make my way over to the bar. With a quick glance downstairs, I notice Savvie and Peyton sitting at one of the booths. They're leaning in, a heated conversation, and I wonder what they're talking about. As if she can feel my eyes on her, Peyton's jade eyes lift to the window. Even though this is one-way glass, I know she sees me. Knows I'm here watching her.

"You stalkin' the lil blondie?" Callan's voice comes from behind me, and I shake my head.

Grabbing two crystal tumblers, I pour a three-finger-deep shot in each of the Scotch Leigh brought me as a gift. Setting one down for Cal, I take a swig of mine.

"She's into you," my brother tells me.

"Don't you think I know that?" I'm angry, frustrated. Running my fingers through my hair for the millionth time today, I recall how she walked out, and also why she walked out. Because I told her to. I gave her the out. Forced it on her.

All the women in my life have come and gone without so much as a blink of my eye. I could so easily turn and find another. I've indulged in countless scenes, with countless women, but somehow, Peyton has turned my world upside down.

"Rick, you're allowed to be happy, you know," Callan tells me. He gulps his drink, and I watch in silence as he pours another. His words are shot directly at my heart. "She's not here anymore. You can't keep living in the past," he says, not looking at me.

I cast a glance down to the club and notice a man in an expensive suit talking to Peyton. My blood burns with jealousy so profuse I can't breathe.

"There comes a time when you need to stop and think, what would happen if that asshole" --my brother gestures with his tumbler at the man I'm shooting daggers at-- "takes her to a room at the back, gives her all she craves and more? Do you think he'll push her away because of his own stupidity?"

"Fuck you, Callan." There are times over the years

my brother has pissed me off. Since we were younger, he's been there, giving me advice. And even though he's older, I've never really listened to him. We fight, we laugh, we drink. The two O'Leary boys have been a force to be reckoned with. "Why do you always have to—"

"Be right?" he interrupts, finishing my question. "Tell me, Rick. Would Rory want you to be angry at the world all the time? Would she want you to be living in the past?"

"I'm not angry at the world, Cal. I'm angry she's gone. That one man took her from me." The raw honesty in my tone is enough to have my throat burning. Fighting with him is second nature. I've never been one to appease my brother, but he's never allowed me to wallow, which is why I respect him. He's given me more than I can ask for, been there for me when I needed him most, and now I feel like an asshole for arguing about this.

"Then we finish this so you can go down there and claim your girl," he tells me easily as if everything is black and white. I wish it was that easy to just walk down there and take Peyton, telling her how I feel. But there's no way I can bring her into my world.

"I can't. She's too good for me. Look what happened to Aurora," I tell him earnestly. He's never seen me cry. I've been broken, but never once did I allow my sadness to show. The steel expression I wore at Rory's funeral showed a man who didn't allow the world to get to him. Not even when he buried the love of his life.

"Look at me, Rick," my brother murmurs, and I do. "Do you love Peyton?"

I took everything from her. And the thing that has my chest tightening is that I gave her something I never wanted to. I allowed her in, and now I know without a fucking doubt I'm falling for her.

"Because, from where I'm standing, brother, you seem to. This girl has given you something, offered you all of her. And from the look on your face, you've given her everything too."

He's right. Every word he utters is the truth. She broke the down the walls I'd built for so long, and as they crumble slowly and effortlessly, I find myself riddled with guilt. I find myself nodding before I can voice the words. The shame that I've moved on from Aurora hits me in the gut, and I know my brother sees it.

"You can't love a ghost. She's gone, and you need to move on." He points at my chest, prodding me, and I know he's trying to get me to see reason. "Your past is just that. Put it behind you. I'm not saying you're going to forget Rory. She'll always be a part of you, but this shit that you're doing to Peyton is wrong."

"I . . . I don't know how to let Rory go." For the first time in years, I feel agony. Real, gut-wrenching agony, and I find myself gripping the glass so tightly I'm willing it to shatter, because this is too much.

"There's only so much anyone can tell you. Only so much advice we can offer. It's your choice, brother. If you ever want to feel a semblance of happiness, you'll say goodbye to Aurora, and let her go now. Nothing can change what happened, but you can change how you deal with it."

"When did you become so wise?"

"The moment my little brother needed me," he smirks. Draining the liquid from his glass, he sets it down and leaves me to wage war with my thoughts. Turning, I watch as Peyton smiles up at the man who could probably love her, give her everything her little heart desires, and I almost walk away. I almost decide to let her go, but then her gaze finds mine through the window.

She's watching me as I watch her. She knows I'm here. Then she darts her gaze away and back to her suitor. Shaking her head, she smiles politely, and he leaves. And in my heart, I wonder if that was her answer. If she's telling me with her actions that she wants me. She wants what I have to offer. But that makes me wonder, what is it that I can offer her?

Shaking my head, I turn to my desk and settle on the chair. I can't hurt her. At least, I can't have her hurt by my enemies. The farther away she is from me, the better. Callan was right. I should move on. And I choose to move on alone. At least, that way, no one can get hurt again.

Years ago, when I was brought into this life, I'd made a choice to spend my existence without casualties. Of course, I broke that promise to myself, and I won't do that again.

The car is almost at the house, and I know soon, I'll see the man who took everything from me. Callan pulls up to the gates, and the first thing I notice is there's no security. Perhaps they're inside.

"Are you ready to get your vengeance? I can do it, if you want me to." My brother has always been there for me. He loves this shit. Stalking, killing, watching someone's life drain from their eyes. The one to do the dirty work because he doesn't mind getting his hands dirty. But this is my fight.

"I just need you to get the evidence," I inform him. My father will need video proof that the man confesses, then watch him die on film. I know it's needed. As much as I know I should do it, I hate knowing I'm going to be forever captured killing someone.

We park on the sidewalk, and I ensure my gun is safely in my holster at the back of my belt. When we exit the car, the scent of freshly mowed grass wafts over to me, and I note there's a neighbor in her garden about four houses down. She doesn't look my way, but being vigilant is always a necessity.

It's late evening. The sun is just disappearing on the horizon as I push open the small pedestrian gate. Strangely, I didn't picture a mobster sitting in a small house in a suburb. But then again, I know he was meant to be lying low.

Callan follows me onto the property. His steps ghosting mine as we head toward the door. My gaze is dragged up to the second floor where a man is standing in the window watching me. He knows. I do too. It's time to finish this.

We make our way to the door. Before I can knock, it opens, and I'm greeted with a maid who is old enough to be my grandmother.

"Hello," she says, her tone wary, the Irish lilt present. It's her eyes that give her away. She knows who I am. Once she steps aside, I enter, and as soon as she shuts the door, he steps out of the shadows.

"Carrick Aiden O'Leary." His brogue is heavy as he calls me by my real name. The accent thick, and it rumbles through me with familiarity.

"Seamus Moran," I respond as he nods, gesturing for me to step inside his space. There's nothing here that suggests he's a murderer, and there's also nothing to give away the fact that he is one of the most dangerous men in Europe, and possibly now in Chicago.

"You've come here to collect your penance," he says easily, settling in the arm chair. He's old. Much older than I thought. I'm confused as to how he is the son of the Moran. "And you didn't expect to see me." He meets my glare easily, not fazed that I've pulled out my gun. The silencer is in place as I watch him, taking in the man who stole lives, countless innocents died because he wanted to rule the fucking country.

Callan has his phone out, recording this to send to our father. I've never been sure what Dad does with the videos, but with each job I've completed in the past, it's been a necessity. The man watches me, gesturing for me to sit. I do. My brother stays standing as he regards the man warily.

"I've come to make sure you pay your dues," I tell him. There's no mercy, but he doesn't ask for it. I drop the barrel, aiming at his left knee and pull the trigger. The anguished cry that's wretched from his mouth is all I need to put another bullet in his other kneecap.

That's when his men appear. Four of them flank him, two on either side of the asshole who's gripping his bloodied legs. The sticky crimson liquid that spurts from the holes I've made oozes as he keels over. His hands holding onto the wounds does nothing to stop the bleeding.

I sit back, settling myself on the sofa as I watch him wallow around the floor. The four men who appeared pull their weapons on me. I don't move. It's best to play cool when you're outnumbered. Callan is silent beside me, but his hand is on his gun, which is in the holster. I notice his phone is gone, and his gaze is trained on the men in the room.

"They say cockroaches never learn. They never die either, but I'm here to ensure that you're on the path straight to hell, Moran," I smirk, crossing my arms in front of my chest as he glares up at me.

"As you know the code we live by, O'Leary. An eye for an eye. This is done. The men behind me will escort you from this house, and I suggest you stay away. I'll move on, back to Ireland, but you're not to follow. Your father will know I've paid with my legs."

"You fucking took her from me!" I roar. Shooting up from the sofa, I make a move to grasp his shirt. The men cock their guns, but he holds a hand up to stop them.

I'm not sure why he's done it, but I continue dragging him over to the sofa where I was sitting. I lean in, taking in his cold green eyes. He doesn't flinch, but he shouldn't. We're both trained killers. We've both tortured men, maimed them. This is child's play compared to what we've seen.

"You killed her," I hiss in his face as my anger finally releases itself. My fists make contact with his face, again and again. I don't see anything but the violent rage that envelops me in its thick fog.

The crunch of bone, the splatter of blood, and the way his body shudders under each violent punch doesn't stop me. I don't know how many times I hit him. I lose track of time. It's only when I finally collapse on the floor do I realize I'm crying.

Callan grips my arm, pulling me to stand. "It's done, brother. We need to leave."

"Remember, O'Leary, there's always a time and place for everything. You've gotten what you came for.

If you ever come near me again, I'll ensure you don't walk out the door."

I should kill him. But the four men behind me will take me out without breaking a sweat. I knew I'd be overpowered. There wasn't a time I didn't think I'd be walking out of here alive, and that's why I let Peyton walk away. I watched the woman I love walk out the door because I knew I wouldn't walk out of this alive.

For years, I've held my agony in my chest. And for years, I've lived with rage and guilt, and revenge that seemed to riddle my heart. But one woman strode in, her blonde hair, green eyes, and sassy mouth broke me. She fucking shattered me, and I realize I love her.

"Callan, wait outside." It's an order. I don't outrank him, but he obeys. Once I'm alone, I pull out my phone and hit the send button on a message. The back door of the house is shattered, as I raise my gun. I didn't want my brother to see this.

My finger presses the trigger as my team appears, and I watch in awe as the man who stole Rory from me slumps. Suddenly, my ears prick at a sound from behind me. I don't have a moment to move because the pain that sears through me is relentless as I slump and black takes over.

Eighteen

Peyton

The room is quiet, lit in a soft yellow glow of the candles.

"Peyton." Oliver's voice startles me when he appears from the entrance in the wall opposite of where I'm standing. "What are you doing here?" He smiles, approaching me with a curious stare. Dressed in a navy pinstripe suit with a crisp white shirt and a tie which matches his suit, he looks like he's about to head into a board meeting.

"I wanted to talk to you." I sound shy and nervous, but I'm not. He took my brother on as a submissive, and even though I never thought of Chance in this lifestyle, I never saw myself in it either. As long as he's happy, I'll support him.

"Of course." Oliver offers me a hand. "Sit, please,

Peyton." He gestures to the chair beside him. "What can I do for you?" His rich, decadent tone is calming, and I know now why he's so alluring for all the submissives who walk into Sins. Carrick may be the man-whore, but it's Oliver who's the older, distinguished man who'll offer anything you want. Being a sadist, he caters to masochists, but his age affords him the perfect Daddy Dom scenario.

"My brother, he's not used to all this, but I just wanted to talk to you about looking after him. I know you will. There's no doubt in my mind, but I was concerned about—"

"Peyton, darling, let me assure you of something. All the subs I've had in my dungeon have come out stronger, surer of themselves, and they've loved every minute I spent with them in there. I don't talk about my relationships."

He settles back, watching me for a moment, and I feel foolish for coming here and asking him about it. Not that I wanted to know what he does, but more that he'll not break Chance's heart.

"This is something I live twenty-four seven. I'm a lot

of things to different people. Yes, I do train many slaves and subs, but I also find myself indifferent to monogamy. If I feel that I want to be with your brother and perhaps another woman, I will do so."

He's silent for a moment longer, giving me time to digest his words.

I nod.

He smiles.

"There's never an easy way of diving into my world. Granted, not all people enjoy the same things, but I'll never hurt someone when they don't want it. I'm not proud of some of the things I've done, but what I do within the walls of my dungeon stays there."

"I'm sorry, I didn't mean to question you." Meeting his steel-gray eyes, I smile.

"I can certainly see why Rick is so enamored with you," he utters almost reverently.

"It was my choice to walk away, but he's moved on," I tell him sadly.

"Oh, sweet Peyton, you have that man by the balls. I've seen Dominants fall for the subs they train, but nothing like Rick and you. What you've found with him is something that doesn't come easy." He sounds so sure of himself I almost believe it. I want to. My heart wants to grab at his words and hold them tight, but I can't allow myself to feel.

"He's . . . complicated."

"Aren't all men complicated?" he quips, his mouth turning up into a grin. The fine wrinkles at the corner of his eyes show his age, along with the silver strands that color his dark hair.

"I suppose they are," I tell him. "But this is different. I mean, he's still in love with his ex. I mean, I look like her. That's why he wanted me in the first place."

"Peyton, has he told you he still loves her?" I shake my head *no*. "So, you're putting words into his mouth that he never once uttered." I nod. "Let me tell you something. A long time ago, when I first became a Master to a beautiful slave, I fell hard. Infatuated with everything about her. She had long brown hair that reminded me of the warmest chocolate, her eyes, the color of roasted chestnuts, and skin that was smooth, tanned, and silky."

He smiles, then pushes off the chair, striding toward

a small cabinet.

"I trained her, fell in love with her, and then she left. Walked out one day without a word. I thought I had done something wrong. Perhaps pushed her past her boundaries. But one night, I walked into Sins. Years later, mind you," he continues as he pours a drink. When he nears me once more, he offers me a glass of a red wine, which smells delicious.

"And she was there?"

He nods. "She was. Hanging off the arm of another Master. When she saw me, she blanched. I didn't go to her, I didn't even acknowledge I'd seen her. Instead, I moved on, but I didn't forget her. When I chose a new slave, she was the spitting image of Anna. I did it to see if it was love or lust. When you love someone in this lifestyle, it's difficult sometimes to distinguish between need and want, to please, and real love."

I'm hooked on every word. My heart thudding against my ribs as I listen to the man who seems to have more heartache shining in his gray eyes than anyone I'd ever met.

"Most submissives and slaves become lost when

they don't have someone who can offer them what they need. They seek it out, and sometimes it's dangerous. The same for a Dominant. He craves that control, and when he loses that, he can end up spiraling, and that's what happened to Rick. When he lost Aurora, he didn't take on another sub the way he did you."

His eyes meet mine. There's a gentle plea in them.

"He may have first chosen to train you because you looked like her, but I don't believe for a second he fell in love with you because of it. Your looks may have cracked his shell, but it was your personality, your fire, who you are as a person that made him love you. When you walked in, you were the reckoning. Either he'd fall for you, Peyton, or he'd have one more chance to say goodbye to the girl with the blonde hair and pretty green eyes. He'd fuck you, spank you, and move on to the next."

"But, he didn't move on. At least, not until I told him I needed time. Learning about the fact that I was just a reminder of this girl he'd lost so long ago hurt."

"Of course, it will hurt. There's no doubt about it. But, what I'm saying is, he fell in love again, so his heart is free. He gave it to you. You may look alike, but you're two very different people. When you love someone, it's not the outer appearance that you love, it's the soul, the heart of that person."

He's right.

"If you really love Carrick, I would suggest you show him. Give him the choice to decide what he wants. However, if you can no longer submit to him, then move on. He's a Dominant. It's his nature, who he is. If he can't have that, he loses himself, and it won't work between you both."

"I just need time. A day or two to think about it."

He nods. Taking my hand in his, he pulls me into his arms. They're warm, almost father like. His spicy scent reminds me of a cold winter's day sitting by the fire with hot chocolate and cinnamon. Oliver plants a chaste kiss on the top of my head.

He takes a step back, meeting my gaze. "You're a good girl, Peyton. You'll both be happy, just don't rush into anything. He'll wait."

"How do you know he will?" I saw Carrick with that woman a few days ago while she sat on his lap draped over him. He saw me, looked into my eyes, and smiled. My heart cracked just a little. But then again, we both played games. I went into the back room with Oliver to make him jealous. But nothing happened, that's a small tidbit Rick doesn't know.

"He'll wait because he loves you. There's no one else he'd rather have kneeling for him."

"And you know that?"

"Because I understand him. We share the same desires, needs, and when a man like me loves, we love for eternity." He sounds so confident and sure. His voice deep, a rumble that vibrates through us both.

"As do I, Oliver," I respond, earning me a smile and a nod. "I do love him. Perhaps it's time I pulled on my big girl panties and went to him."

"You need to be very sure it's what you want. But I know my friend, he's not going to push or force you into anything. However, if you walked in there right now, I assure you, he'd take you back this instant. And I know that he's not been with anyone since. He has taken subs to the rooms, but I know he hasn't been inside any woman since you."

"You can't know that for sure."

"I can, darling," he assures me.

"Thank you for everything, Oliver." I smile, leaning up on my tip-toes, I plant a soft kiss on his cheek. The stubble that dusts it tickles my lips. "I appreciate everything."

He releases me. I turn to leave, but before I have time to leave the room, Oliver calls to me. "If you ever need anything, Peyton, I'm here for you."

Nodding, I smile up at him. "Thank you."

NINETEEN

CARRICK

I open my eyes to find Callan slumped in the chair under the window. The white fluorescent lights are blinding. There's an ache in my chest, which grips my lungs painfully. Breathing is difficult. I want out of this fucking hospital bed.

I try to shuffle up, but the agony that shoots through me is excruciating.

"Cal," I croak. My throat burns. "Callan," I call again, causing my brother to jerk up and stare at me. "I need water." He moves quickly, pouring some from the jug at the foot of my bed.

"I thought I'd lost you there, brother."

"You can't get rid of me that easy," I retort, wincing at the burning in my throat.

He hands me the cup. "Be nice to me, or you won't

get out of here."

"What did they say? I want to go home." He nods in understanding. He's been in this position a few times before. Nothing like this, but I've had to break him out of the hospital when the doctors wanted to keep him drugged up for no reason.

Callan and I grew up hard. We didn't need to be coddled. If one of us got hurt, we would get up, dust ourselves off, and move along, and that's what I want to do.

"I need to talk to you before though," Callan starts. When I meet his gaze, I have a feeling I know what this is about. Peyton.

"I don't want to hear it, Cal."

"You don't want to, but you have no choice but to listen." I sigh, because he's right. Nodding, I wait for him to continue. "She believes you love her because she looks like Rory."

"How do you know?" I question, frowning at his assessment of the woman I do love.

"I'm not stupid, Rick. I've been finding out information on people for a long time, and this is no different. I can tell. The thing is, I know it's not true. So, I'm going to talk to her."

"No."

We've reached an impasse. He wants to tell Peyton to fight for me when I didn't fight for her. She saw me with another woman, and that's when she went to Oliver. I didn't have a right to be angry, but I was. More than I thought I could be.

Jealousy is something I'd never dealt with, but with Peyton, it burns through me. Not only thinking about her with another man, but seeing her with Oliver set off something inside me. I'm being unreasonable. I can't have her, so no other man can. It's wrong. I shouldn't do that to her, but I can't help it.

"You love her," he states, settling back in the chair. "She loves you. This is a ridiculous game of cat and mouse you're both playing, Rick. Why not just be a man and tell her? Grow some fucking balls, man."

All my life, my brother has been the strong one. He's also been the one to fix shit. And I know he's trying to do that now with Peyton. I should thank him. He's right. I need to man up. She deserves someone who'll not only fight for her, but someone who will kill for her.

That's me.

"Are you going to let me help you fix this shit you got yourself into?" His question stills me. *Do I?* If I allow him to get Peyton to give me a second chance, will I be able to give her everything she needs from me? I want to.

"She'll never take me back. She saw me in Sins with that chick on my lap and lost her shit." His eyes narrow at my words. He shakes his head in disappointment. I feel it right down to my bones. He sighs then pushes up from the chair.

"I'm heading out to see Madison," he tells me, but he doesn't meet my eyes. He's lying. I've learned my brother's nuances a long while ago. When he tells me something and can't meet my eyes, I know he's bullshitting me.

"If you go near Peyton—"

"Fuck off, Rick. I'll be back in a few hours. I need to release some tension, and that means I get to fuck that sweet little cunt of the precious Madison Parker," he smirks devilishly.

"You're an asshole. Her father is going to—"

"Her father won't do shit to me. I'll kill him before he even blinks my way. The asshole is a prim and proper pussy, and you know what I do with pussies. I fuck them up until they're bleeding pretty crimson."

He winks as he makes his way to the door.

"And don't forget," he says before leaving. "You and Peyton need to sort your shit out, so don't go dying on me." And then he's out the door. Shaking my head, I lie back and stare at the ceiling. He's right. As much as I don't want to admit it, I know he's right.

Fuck.

TWENTY

PEYTON

The night is silent. The moon hangs high in the inky sky. Stars twinkle as I watch the sky turn a dark shade of navy, then turn to black. My feet are perched on the railing of the balcony. I'm sipping a glass of wine, and I'm trying not to think about Carrick, Oliver, and everything that's happened over the past few weeks.

The memory of losing myself in a man like Rick is like stealing my breath, leaving me flailing for air. And the problem is, he's the only one who can give it back to me. My heart aches for what I lost. What I chose to walk away from, and what both of us had fucked up.

The doorbell buzzes, dragging me from my thoughts of a man better left in my past. Heading to the door, I peek through the peephole to find Callan. There's something far darker about Carrick's brother. His demeanor, his personality, and the way he carries himself.

He's dangerous, and I know it. Yes, they're both sons of a mob boss, but Callan is different. I pull the door open to meet his seductive smirk. The dark dusting of stubble on his chin is vastly different to the smooth jaw of Carrick.

"What are you doing here?"

He doesn't wait for me to invite him in. Instead, he pushes past me into the apartment.

"You can't just—"

"Rick's in the hospital." His words cause my heart to stutter. My lungs don't work as I try to pull in air. "He's fine." Callan turns to regard me. "I figured you'd want to know."

"What happened?" I shut the door with my eyes on the man before me. I can't help but shiver at the thought of Rick hurt. Or worse. Shoving the thought away, I move into the living room where Callan has settled himself on the sofa.

He looks out of place here. My feminine furniture with his rugged appearance is like black and white. His eyes pin me to the spot, rooting me in place.

"He was shot. The bullet grazed through him. He'll be out soon. I wanted to talk to you about something, and I wanted to do it without my brother around."

I settle on the corner of my sofa, my legs pulled up under me, and I don't miss the way Callan's eyes shoot to the spot where my heels meet my ass. His mouth quirks. His gaze darkens considerably. "My brother and I never really saw eye to eye. All the years we've been doing this shit, I've been the one who loved it. He never did. This is something I wanted for my life. Killing people, it's in my blood. My nature is to see the life drain from them."

He stops for a moment, and I'm certain he can see the shock on my face. There's a raw honesty to him, blatant and unapologetic. I wonder if he's ever been in love. It's a stupid thought, and once more, I have to squash it down where my love for Carrick hides.

"Rick is a man who wants a family. When I saw him and Rory together, I knew that being a killer wasn't what he was cut out for. He's a business man. He enjoys running the club, and when he needed to kill Moran today, I saw him flinch."

"He killed someone?" The question comes out in

a breathy gasp. Shock lacing every word. I knew what Carrick does. He told me. But the thought of him actually killing someone is different to just the idea of him doing it.

"No. Carrick couldn't do it. There's where the problem lies, Peyton. If he lives the life my father wants for him, he'll be dead with no questions asked. And you know why? Because he loves someone. It's an emotion that makes men weak."

"Rick is far from weak," I bite out, moving closer to the man who's angered me. He doesn't flinch. He chuckles at my outburst. "Perhaps because you've never loved someone, you don't know, but I believe that love makes people stronger than anything else."

"You're a woman who loves him. Of course you'd say that. When you're in this business, pretty girl, you can't flinch. You can't second guess yourself. And that's what happened today. He did it, and I only realized in that moment why he would ever allow himself to die."

"Why?" I blink, tears fall. My heart, which I shut away, leaps into action, wanting to go to Carrick and make things right.

"He believes he doesn't deserve you. He's convinced that because of his past, because of Rory, you shouldn't be with him. And you know what? I agree. I don't want my brother to die over pussy. He can get it anywhere he wants, but for some godforsaken reason, he wants you."

Shaking my head, I rise from the sofa and pad into the open-plan kitchen. Grabbing a mug, I fill it with coffee, then I pour a double shot of Jameson whiskey into a tumbler and join Callan again. Handing him the alcohol, I settle in the same spot and watch as he downs the drink in one gulp.

He doesn't even wince when he swallows. The man is a beast.

"He wanted me because I reminded him of Aurora. He said I looked like her."

His gaze lands on me. He watches me, not just my hands trembling, or the slight trickle of tears on my cheeks, but he sees my heart. It's as if he's trying to reach into my chest and rip it from its cage.

He rises, heads to the cabinet, and lifts the bottle in gesture. I nod. He pours another shot and joins me once more. "Thank you, little lady," he smirks, gulping it down like it's water.

"You're welcome."

"He doesn't want you because you look like Rory." I watch him, furrowing my brows in confusion. That's what Carrick told me. I look like her. He chose me because I reminded him of her. "You see, when Rory died, Rick told me something before he left. He said that one day, he'll come across a woman, it didn't matter what she looked like, but she'll make him love again."

I'm trying to breathe. I'm trying not to cry. But I can't stop.

"He said that when she comes along, he'll know. I, of course, told him he's full of shit. And even a few days ago in his office, I still had a feeling he was holding on to a ghost, and I told him that much, but he was adamant it wasn't the reason you were in his life. I've only ever seen Carrick that confident once before. The day he moved here. He knew what he wanted, and he went for it. You see, I don't ever believe my brother loved Aurora the way he loves you, because with her, he was what our family would say is destined to be together. An arranged marriage, so to speak. With you, it was natural. It was real."

I gape at him for a long while. We sit in silence. He swirls the nonexistent liquid in his glass while I grip the mug so tightly my hands burn from the liquid. I don't know what to say or how to even fathom how much I fucked this up. I asked for time. I got jealous when I saw him with another woman.

"I love him," I tell Callan. He nods as if he knew that all along. "Is that why you came here?" Once again, his head moves in ascent. "I've fucked it up."

"You couldn't lose that man even if you tried. If there's one thing you need to learn about my brother, it's that he's a stubborn ass. When he wants something, he doesn't give up easily."

"He told me he'd never stop fighting for my heart, but Callan, he hasn't been by here to fight. He hasn't given me any reason to believe he wants this. Wants me."

He watches me for a little while before he smiles. "He has been a bit of an asshole, but I want you to know, he loves you more than anything, or anyone. If you feel that he's your *one,* then I suggest you go there and you make sure he knows it. Because right now, he's just being an asshole."

"He is," I agree.

He chuckles. I watch as he rises to full height, but before he can leave I ask him something I wanted to voice earlier. "Why did you come here?"

"You needed to know my brother may be a stubborn dick at times, but he's not a bad man. He's so far from it."

"Are you the bad man?"

He doesn't respond with words, only offers me a chuckle before he pulls the door open and leaves my apartment.

The golden sunshine that streams through the windows wakes me from a dream of Carrick, a leather whip, and a few million orgasms. Okay, maybe not a million, but there were too many to count.

After Callan's visit last night, I called Savvie and Chance. I want to go shopping. I need the perfect outfit to wear tonight when I go and see Rick. Callan said he'd be out of the hospital and back at work. Even though the doctor told him to take it easy, I know he'll never listen to someone telling him how to live his life.

My time with Rick has changed me. It's cemented in my mind who and what I am. As much as I never believed it, I know without a doubt I'm his. He's owned me since the moment he kissed me.

And every day since then, I've only been here for him.

He played me like a musical instrument.

He showed me pleasure and pain.

And now, I've got to show him I'm no longer scared. I have to give him the one thing he's wanted all along. He was just too afraid to ask me for it, and I was too scared to give it.

I may have submitted the few times we did play, but never like this. I want him to have me. All of me. The parts I never showed anyone before, even the pain I'd experienced as a child, I want him to know me.

I know now that I found him for a reason. I was meant to be with him. Our paths crossed for me to learn from him, and that's why I couldn't move on. I couldn't bring myself to be with another man. Even though so much time has passed since he last touched me, kissed me, held me in his arms, he's still there. Inside me. My heart soars at the realization. My chest is no longer tight with fear and anxiety. And the tears have stopped.

I head into the shower, turning on the taps. Quickly, I strip down and step under the spray. Tiny prickles of lukewarm water cascade down my body. I pick up the orchid body wash I bought a couple of days ago and lather my skin with the silky liquid. The scent of the flowers fills the small steamy space, and it takes me back to the moment I first walked into Carrick's home.

I make quick work of rinsing off then toweling myself dry when I step back into my bedroom. I decide on a pair of jeans and a bright pink flowy T-shirt that hangs just below my ass. I slip my feet into my sandals and make my way into the kitchen.

"Baby girl." My brother's voice comes from my living room entrance, causing me to glance into familiar eyes as if I'm looking into a mirror. "You needed a shopping partner?" He smiles. It's bright and carefree. He's not mentioned Oliver again, but I have a feeling there's more to their friendship than my brother has let on.

"I do. It's time I went to my man. I want him, Chance. All these stupid fears that held me back only stopped me from having what I want and need."

"I'm happy for you, Peyton. If he is the one who makes you smile, then I'll have to overlook what he did with those other girls."

"He wasn't with them. I spoke to Oliver, and Callan was here last night as well. They've both confirmed Rick hasn't actually been with anyone." My brother's eyebrows shoot up in surprise. His face is a picture of shock and elation. And I'm sure I looked the same way when Callan told me how much his brother loves me.

I sigh, knowing my brother isn't going to let this go. His hand on my shoulder is evidence enough of that. "If he ever hurts you. I'll kill him." A giggle escapes my lips at my Chance's vow, and I nod. "I meant it, Pey."

"I know." I wrap my arms around his middle, needing his safety for a moment. The way my brother cares for me always made me feel special. Now I have two men who love me, and I feel like a princess.

"You know what, sugar plum? I've only got one

sister, and I need to make sure she's happy. And I have to tell you all about Oliver. We can gossip on the way to the store." Chance leans in, his mouth on my cheek. "I can't believe how intense that man is. Utterly, beautifully, filthy, but exquisite in every way."

"Seriously, Chance?" I retort, playfully slapping his shoulder. "I don't want to know about my brother fucking."

"Why not?" He winks. We've always been honest with each other. And this will be no different. As long as there are no graphic details, I'll be fine.

"You drive me crazy. I can't believe you're here. Will you stay?" I question hopefully. Perhaps now that Chance has a reason to stay, he'll be able to move his stuff in and spend time in Chicago.

"Oliver said he'd love for me to stay. He wants to see me more often. I'm not sure how it's going to work because Leigh is there too." He seems to be considering this as he speaks. "She's beautiful, delicious."

"Oh my God, have you had like . . . I mean . . . Are you?"

"There's a lot we need to work through, but I'm in

a relationship with them both. It's exciting. I'm happy, Pey." His words have me grinning like an idiot.

"Just watch your heart. I know you end up smitten like this and then get in way over your head." It's a sisterly warning which he needs to hear. I've seen Chance with a broken heart. It's not pretty.

"Don't worry about me. You need to worry about yourself, baby girl." He gives me a kiss on the cheek, and I nod.

"You're my brother. Worrying is something that comes naturally."

"Let's go shopping," he declares, pulling me into the living room as the door to my apartment opens, and I find Savannah dressed in a pair of jean cutoffs and a purple tank top.

"Let's get this party started."

The three of us giggle as we make our way out the door.

My stomach is a flurry of excitement and I just hope that Carrick is still waiting for me when I get to him.

TWENTY ONE

CARRICK

After my talk with Callan, I haven't had the balls to call her.

The pain in my chest has nothing to do with the gunshot that grazed my vital organs. The pain ebbs and flows. I shouldn't have the alcohol with my pain meds, but I can't help it. I'm doing it to stop the agony of losing Peyton.

The night is hot, humid, and heavy with want. Sins is packed to the rafters with beautiful women and good-looking men. There's an energy that drips from the pores of every person in here. Mason and Savvie are at the bar, but I don't see Peyton. She's been here a handful of times since she walked out, and that's when I tend to steer clear of the main area of the club.

She made her choice. She walked out when I bared

my fucking soul. She left me cold and barren, and that's the asshole I now play. Heartless and domineering. I pass by the bar, lifting a finger toward Dylan who's pouring drinks for a couple. His gaze flits to me. He nods in acknowledgment. Seconds later, a tumbler of gin and tonic is sitting on the counter for me.

Giggling from the corner booth grabs my attention, and I turn to find two brunettes sitting together. I don't think twice as I take my drink and make my way over to them. The soft sounds of their whispers and gentle giggles cause my blood to heat. Since I've been single, I've attempted to go back to who I was before Peyton by indulging once more. The problem is, each time I take a woman to my playroom, there's only one face in my mind and I can't go through with it.

"Ladies," I murmur, lowering my voice so only they can hear me. Both sets of eyes drag to me, taking me in from head to toe. "I trust you're having a good evening thus far?"

"Thank you, yes," one of them responds. Her cheeks turning a soft shade of pink.

"How about you and your friend join me for a

scene?"

Their gazes dart to each other in surprise. Lifting my glass to my lips while waiting for a *yes*, I take a long sip of the alcohol. I may be overly confident, but they look like they could be ready to drop to their knees right here.

"That would be lovely," the other one smiles.

"And your names?" I quip, watching as she blushes as well. The color turning my cock to steel behind the metal zipper of my slacks.

"I'm Amy, and this is Lyra," she introduces herself and her friend.

Both women are beautiful, with not much make-up and big brown eyes I can already picture tearing up as I feed them both my cock.

"Good," I respond. "Get the barman to escort you to my playroom. He'll know which one." I turn to walk away, lifting my glass to Dylan with a slight nod. His response is a knowing smile. My gaze is torn from before me to the staircase where I find Peyton glaring at me.

She chose to walk away. To tell me it's over. I'm only doing what I've always done. Fuck and dominate.

Stalking into the room, I set down my tumbler and shrug off my jacket. The bed has been set up with cuffs on the headboard, which I'll be using in a few moments.

Grabbing the whip, I set it on the nightstand. I strike a match, lighting three pink candles. Once the soft orange glow offsets the shadows in the bedroom, I settle in the armchair with my drink. The room itself has a bar, so if I really wanted to get fucked up tonight, I can.

The door slides open, and both women walk in dressed all in black. The lingerie that hugs their curves is mouthwatering. Nothing, and I mean no fucking woman can compare to Peyton, but this is what she chose.

"Amy, I want you on the bed. On your back. Lyra, cuff her to the headboard," I order gruffly, while palming my cock through my slacks. The women move without uttering a response. Such good submissives. Not feisty like the blonde who currently holds my heart. They're not a challenge. Anything I ask them to do, they'll obey.

"Lyra, take off that bra. I want your tits out." She reaches around to unclasp the black lace. Once it pools on the floor, she places both hands on her tits, lifting them, tweaking the nipples until she whimpers from the bite of pain. "Panties next," I utter, draining my glass with my eyes glued to her movements. Once she's naked, I set the tumbler down. Crooking my finger, I call her to me.

"Yes, Sir?" she mumbles. Her voice tentative, nervous, and I can't help smiling.

"I want you on that bed, between Amy's thighs. You've eaten cunt before. Haven't you?" I question, my mouth quirking into a smirk when her eyes widen.

"I-I . . . no, Sir." Her whisper grates on my nerves, but her smooth cunt is all I need.

"Get on the fucking bed," I bite out, my blood heating with anger, frustration.

She moves quickly, settling herself between her friend's thighs. I watch as she slides Amy's panties down. Then, she leans in and kisses her friend in the most intimate area.

"Good girl," I utter the two words every submissive would want to hear. I'm being an asshole. This is who I've always been. Uncaring. Cold. And right now, I can't do much more to prove that I'm anything else. I tried. I gave Peyton everything, and I still lost. The one woman who finally showed me that love was possible. That my heart wasn't cold and barren. As soon as I opened myself to her and I offered her the truth, she walked out.

She fucking ran.

"I'm not going to go easy on you, Lyra," I tell the pretty brunette.

Her gaze darts up, her mouth wet with the arousal from her friend. "I want it," she utters, and I know I've chosen well.

The thought has me rising from my seat, stalking to the two girls. I lift the whip, raising it in the air with a loud swish, then bring it down on Lyra's ass. The resounding swat echoes, and her screams are music to my ears. I'm punishing her for what Peyton did, and I can't fucking stop myself.

Again and again, like a savage, I rain down the leather on the tanned flesh of the woman who's currently whimpering into her friend's cunt. Rabid anger races through my body when I see the welts rising on her flesh.

Dropping the whip, I shove my slacks down and sheath my cock. But I don't do what I'm tempted to. I want to sink into Lyra's tight cunt, but my heart stops me. It fucking grips me, causing the breath to leave my lungs. I fist my cock, fucking it as I watch the two women do my bidding.

I'm an asshole.

I'm a fucking prick.

I hate myself and my needs. I hate that I hurt Peyton. Allowing her to see me with someone else made sure I fucked everything up. She'll never want me again. I jerk my dick, faster and faster.

"Fuck her cunt with those fingers. Make her scream," I bite out. My anger surges along with my desire as I feel the deep pull inside me. Harder and faster. My hand rains down a spank, causing extra marks to form on her already marred flesh. I can't rein in my control. It's unleashed, and my body moves of its own volition. My hips slam into my hand.

Her screams are louder now as I spank her almost violently. She's moaning, begging, as it mingles with the sound of sex. Pure unadulterated filth. I want Peyton. I love Peyton. But my body has shut down.

My eyes shut tight. I see her, the blonde beauty who stole everything from me.

Again, all I see is Peyton Moore.

"Rick." My name echoes through the haze. I blink. Once. Twice. My heart aches. I hear her. I hear Peyton, but I know it's a lie. I've seen her, heard her, fucking imagined her for weeks, and each time I believed she'd come back, it was nothing more than my mind playing tricks on me.

"Take it," I growl. My hand stinging with agony as I mark the porcelain skin, seeing the welts rising in bright red. I know I'm bruising her, but I don't care. Because that's the type of asshole I am.

"Carrick!"

The scream of my name shatters me in that moment. I empty my seed into the rubber I almost fucked into another woman. Turning, I find the blonde beauty at the door watching me jerk off with two other women. Her big green eyes are wide, glistening with agony and unshed tears.

Her mouth opens, then closes as she takes in the scene before me. Two women, my softening cock in my hand.

"Peyton," I utter her name in surprise when I finally find my voice. She looks like an angel, an apparition sent to destroy me, which she's already done. I'm off the bed, tugging my slacks up when she turns to leave. With a quick glance behind me, I know what I have to do.

Racing from the room, I find her standing in the hallway. Tears stream down her face. Her body is wracked with sobs as she chokes on her emotion. My lungs are once more attempting to draw in breath, but I can't because it hurts too much. She's walking away again, because I've fucked up.

"You . . . What are you doing here?" I lean in, whispering the words over her cheek. I inhale her for a moment, reveling in her scent. I've missed her. It's like not having air for so long and suddenly my lungs are full.

Her body trembles against me. Her eyes peeking up at me as she regards me. She's nervous. I'm nervous too. I want to kiss her. I want to fucking claim her. I've wanted to since the moment I saw her in the darkened hallway.

I realized it wasn't because she reminded me of Rory, it was because it was her. Those pretty green eyes that lured me in like a siren. She took everything from me that day—my attention, my smile, and my heart.

Her gaze drops for a moment. She watches her hands tremble, and she regards them. Then she lifts her gaze to mine, meeting my worried stare. "I came back for you." Her confession sends heat through me, tingling down my spine.

Five words. My resolve cracks. My heart stutters. The ache in my chest turns to a tightening emotion clawing its way up to my throat, thickening. It threatens to choke me. To kill me, because I watch the woman who has my heart in her hands crying.

"Why?" The word falls from my lips before I have time to comprehend what this means. Why she came back. She should've stayed away. She knows I'm bad for her. That's what she told me. "I'm not good for you, Peyton. You have to stay away from me."

"I tried," she whispers with sadness hanging on every word.

"What?" I sound idiotic. One-word questions, but I feel as if fate is playing a cruel joke on me. "I mean, what do you mean?"

"I tried staying away, but what you said about us .

. ." Her words trail off, and I recall our last conversation. I remember the moment I realized I loved her. When I told her three words I vowed never to say to anyone, and she turned away. I didn't blame her. "But you seem to be busy with your friends in there," she bites out, fire burning in her eyes.

Is it bad that I love when she's angry? When all her anger is racing through her like a wildfire, threatening to take me out in its heated blaze?

"That," I gesture toward the door, realizing it might seem as if I'd moved on, but I didn't. I could never replace Peyton. "That's nothing. I needed to forget you, and I tried. Fuck, I tried." I reach for her, but she pushes me away, shoving me backward.

"Don't. I came here because I love you, Carrick, not to watch you fuck other women." The venom in her voice is blazing hot, molten lava dripping over my heart. She prods my chest, causing me to retreat against the wall. I allow her to continue her tirade. Watching in awe as my woman fights me. "You didn't need me ten minutes ago when you were watching them fuck each other," she grits out through clenched teeth, her eyes are filled with fire. "I'm not a fucking toy, Carrick. I'm yours. Do you understand what I gave you?" Her voice rises, and I can't take it anymore. "Fuck you, Carrick Anderson. Fuck you and your—"

Gripping her shoulders, I spin her around and pin her against the wall. She fights against me, pushing and clawing at me, but I don't allow her to move. "You will stop this, right fucking now. Do you understand me, Kitten?"

"Let me go!"

"No, not until you stop fighting me," I inform her, my lips brushing along the lobe of her ear. She sighs, but I don't let her go. My hands trail down her arms. Finding her hips, I hold her steady and press my erection against her ass. "You feel that, baby? That's yours. Every part of me is yours. I do love you, Peyton."

"Let go of me, Carrick, or I swear to god, I will knee you in the balls when I turn around." Her threat causes me to chuckle, but I let her breathe. Stepping back, I watch as she turns to face me.

"If I ever, and I mean ever, see you near another woman again—"

"There will never be another woman. Because you're the only one I want."

"So, they didn't get you hard?" she quips with a bite of jealousy and anger twirling side by side, her chin gesturing to the door that's still closed.

"No. I was stroking my cock imagining how good you'd look being eaten out by another girl. I was picturing you bound to that bed while both women pleasured you. But as soon as I wanted to touch them, it was you who I wanted in there with me, taking my cock like you were made to. Peyton, I love you. I need you to understand that."

She nods. Her face a picture of happiness. She tangles her fingers in mine, tugging me toward the club. I'm about to protest when she turns toward the stairs, taking them two at a time. I'm not sure what she's doing, but I follow. Like a man lost at sea, I allow her light to guide me as if she's my lighthouse in the dark.

We reach my office, and she shoves the door open.

"Peyton," I whisper her name with confusion in my tone. I watch in awe as she slips the slinky straps of the pink dress she's wearing over her shoulders. It pools to the floor, and my breath catches in my throat.

Her lace underwear is see-through. There's a small tattoo above the waistline of her panties. She smiles when she looks down, her fingers tracing the letters reverently. Then, she kneels. She drops down, her thighs parted slightly. Her hands, palms up holding onto my favorite paddle. I've not used it on her yet, but this is her, submitting, giving me her all.

"Eyes up," I command, watching her raise her chin. "You got a tattoo without my permission?" I question. Her eyes widen in shock. She didn't realize that all permanent changes to her body are my decision to make.

"I-I . . ." She shakes her head. "I thought you'd like it." Her tentative voice is filled with confusion. She's pleased me more than she can ever know. But I like to test her. To see how far she's willing to go. If ever I see an ounce of real fear in her eyes, I'll stop. But for now, we're playing.

"It does please me that you wear my brand, Kitten," I confirm, watching her body sag in relief. "However, there's a time and place where you need to ask permission. Tell me, is this it? We're doing this?" I'm unsure of myself. For the first time in a long while, I feel excited by the prospect of finding a long-term sub, but also, I know I'll fuck up more times than I can count, and I need her to stay beside me. Not run and hide.

"I'm giving you me, Sir. I want this. I want you. I ran because I was afraid that I couldn't ever live up to *her* memory. There was pain in my heart that I couldn't deal with while you were around. I thought that each time you look at me, fuck me, spank me, you're wishing I was her. And it hurt."

Her words are honest, raw, dripping with every emotion under the sun, and I know I am to blame. I didn't explain myself to her the first time. I should've given her more of who I was in the beginning rather than hiding.

"You are mine now, Peyton," I growl, low and feral. It's a commanding confirmation.

"Yes, I am. But I need your honesty as much as you need mine, Sir," she bites back.

"You will have it," I affirm with confidence. I'm tired of us being apart when we were always meant to be together. I was just too blind to see it. It's time we make things right. It's time to finally admit how we really feel for each other. And I may not have a collar for her yet, but soon, I'll put one around her neck and properly claim her.

My mind is awash with things I want to do to her right now. To hurt her, make her cry with pleasure, to fuck her until she's limp from orgasms. She'd look beautiful wearing my welts. But it's the tattoo she has on her left hip that makes me smile. I can't wait to see her wearing my ring and my collar.

I don't want to play here, so I scoop her up and walk her up to my apartment.

Where she belongs.

Twenty Two

Peyton

He sets me down on the sofa, his eyes boring into me as if I'm naked before him. I always feel exposed with him looking at me like that. I'm open to him. My chest is cracked wide, and I allow him to see me. My pain. My fear. And the anxiety of everything that's hit me the past few weeks.

We sit in silence for a while as if we're both waiting for the other person to speak first. Perhaps I want him to confess the pain he lived with while I was gone. Maybe I want to tell him how much I wanted to run into his arms. Or even the moment I saw him in the room with two other women, how the anger had erupted from me, but I don't tell him because all I want is for this to stop.

I want our stupid decisions to stop and for us to finally get back on the right path. Back to each other where we are meant to be. His fingers reach for mine as he takes my hand, brings it to his mouth, and presses kisses to my knuckles, then my palms. He takes his time. His lips feather over my wrists, up my arms, until he reaches my shoulders.

"What are you doing?" I question, watching his lips move along my skin causing goosebumps to rise all over my body.

"Loving you."

Two words have my heart leaping into my throat. He continues his worship of my body with his mouth, licking, kissing, and stroking. He doesn't touch my pussy. He focuses on my breasts, my stomach. His tongue dips into my belly button, making me giggle.

"You know, you never went away," he utters, his mouth at my ear once more. The heat of his breath fanning over my skin. "No matter how much I drank, who I took to those rooms." His whisper is pained. With his thumb, he swipes away my tears. The emotion that trickles down my cheeks for the man I love. "You were always there even when you walked away, Peyton. For years, I was closed off, shut away from the world before me. I spent my time in the dark, hidden behind walls I put up," he whispers, confesses, as if I'm here to offer him salvation.

I cup his face in my hands, reveling in the soft smattering of stubble on his prominent jaw. Chiseled to perfection. He stares at me, meeting my eyes with those gentle golden orbs that see my soul. I open my mouth to speak, but his finger presses my lips, ordering me wordlessly to be quiet.

"I've never allowed anyone inside, and you burrowed your way into my heart," he continues. His voice is low, husky, and ragged. "I never fucked anyone after you. I jerked off watching them."

I wince at his confession, but this is what I wanted. Honesty.

"They were merely toys. Nothing ever filled the void you left. I was half a man for so long, when you walked into my life, I finally felt whole. Losing you was the worst thing I'd been through after Rory." This time he drops his gaze, resting it on our entwined hands. The emotion that hangs so heavy between us is stifling.

"Carrick, you don't have to—"

"You make me whole, Peyton. You are my other half. There's nothing I can say to prove it more than--" he lifts his gaze to mine. It burns into me. It scorches me with emotion. It ignites yearning throughout my body. "I love you, and I will do all I can, for the rest of my life, to ensure you believe that you are made for me."

My eyes flit over his, then his face, mouth, neck. His Adam's apple bobs as he swallows. He's nervous. I lift my stare back to his. Golden pools of honey shimmering with . . . fear? He's afraid. I broke him by walking away, and in the process, I broke myself too.

"I didn't want to love you. I'd convinced myself that it was never in the cards for me. But you, you've changed my mind. As much as I wanted to push, you pulled. And now I'm the one pulling," he tells me earnestly. "Let me pull, Peyton. Please?"

A man who held onto control all this time has finally cracked, and I'm the cause of it. My heart lurches with agony when I realize he really does love me.

"It's time I told you why I ran," I utter, my throat raspy, burning with emotion. The lump in my throat thickens, choking me with the truth of what I'd learned.

"You scared me. Not what happened between us, but more the idea of what you'd done. I judged you when I had no right to," Peyton says as she settles beside me on the sofa. Her body is trembling, but it's not pleasure on her face, it's fear.

"You know you can tell me anything," he assures me, taking my hand in his larger one.

"My ex-fiancé, Michael, was working with the mafia in New York. I knew but ignored it. I . . ." I sigh sadly. His brows furrow in confusion, but I continue with my confession. "I let him be because my father wanted us together. It was only when I turned eighteen that I found out what my father really did."

His golden eyes pierce mine. He looks into my soul and implores me to believe he's not the same. I see it. And I do. It's as if he can read my mind.

"Being a loan shark for the mob was his undercover job. The one he never wanted us to know about, but . . ." I trail off. My tone is sad yet frustrated. "I figured it out. I walked in on a meeting he was having, and Michael, being his right-hand man, escorted me out. That was the first time I saw his true colors. The man I was in love with." I glance at Carrick as I tell him, but I can tell he's not angry. There's not even and inkling of jealousy on his handsome face because he must know without a doubt I am his. "He was a liar, just like my father."

"I'm not him." Once again, he assures me, and I nod.

"I know. I was scared, because that night, Michael and I went out, and two men grabbed me. They . . . they would've hurt me because of who Michael worked for and what he was to the mob."

I shake my head sadly. His eyes shimmer as they regard me. He doesn't interrupt me, for which I'm grateful. I want to get this out as easily as possible.

He takes my other hand in his, drawing my attention to his face as he places a kiss on my knuckles. "I'm out of that life, and Callan will be staying here in Chicago to ensure we're safe. My brother is my lifeline, and he'll be yours too."

"The man I was engaged to for years was working for a criminal organization, and I didn't want that life. My heart aches for a family. For kids. Raising them in a house with violence as a norm is not what I envisioned for myself, but then you came along and made me love you."

He smiles. His hands grip mine painfully, but I don't flinch. I want to feel. It's the pain that makes everything real. It ensures I'm still alive.

"I ran from you, but when I saw what it was like living without you, I knew I couldn't do it."

"Peyton, I'm not that man anymore. I've walked away from that life, and my family knows it. Callan and Cayleigh are here to see me. Not to take me back to that life."

"I know. Callan came to see me," I tell him. He doesn't seem shocked, and I wonder if he asked his brother to talk to me. I smile when I recall what Callan said. "I know what you need. I spoke to Oliver about the lifestyle, and he explained it to me."

"What do you mean?"

Sighing, I drop to my knees, needing to do this the right way. I meet his gaze. "You need the control, and I need the submission. I want to please you. It's like an ache deep inside me, like my soul wants to see you happy. It craves the words *good girl* from you. No one else. When I was with Oliver, he told me that I can attempt to be with another man, but I'll never feel the satisfaction I did with you because I love you."

"Peyton—"

"You see, Sir. I'd already given you all of me. Even when I wasn't with you, I was still yours. Nothing could've changed that. I find my strength as a woman in my submission to you."

I smile. I offer him my happiest fucking megawatt grin, and I know without a doubt I'm ready to marry him right now.

"I know. I saw it the moment you kneeled for me in my office all those weeks ago. It may not be a long time that we've been together. But I feel you, Kitten," he coos, pressing three fingers to my chest. "Here."

I swallow past the lump of emotion in my throat. "And I feel you here," I respond, mimicking his action with one of my own. He smiles then. It's bright, beautiful, and makes his face light up. His eyes flicker as if a light has been turned on behind them.

He lifts me in his arms, allowing me to wrap my legs around his waist. "I want to make love to you, then I want to fuck you. When I'm done, you'll not be able to walk, talk, or even feel anything other than my dick inside your body."

I smile at his words. If only he knew how much he was inside me even when he wasn't even near me. "Is that all, Sir?" I purr like a kitten in his ear causing a shudder to travel over his body.

"And don't you ever run away from me again."

"Why?" I sass. "You going to stalk me?"

"I'll do so much more than that. Remember, Kitten, I have rope, cuffs, and many other implements to keep you here." I glance at him, and I know for a fact he's not joking, but I know he'll do anything for me.

"All I need is you." I tell him honestly. And in this moment, I know I'm finally home.

He doesn't respond. He places me on the bed, spreads my legs, and rips my panties from my hips. The bite of pain from the material stings, but I revel in it. He kneels between my legs. His tongue lashes my pussy in long licks. I'm mewling in seconds, but he doesn't relent. His fingers dip and delve into me.

Glancing down, I meet his stare and smile. He's beautiful, even when all I see are those hungry eyes between my legs. He's mouth latches on, suckling my core like I'm his sustenance. I cry out. My fingers tangle in his unruly hair, pulling him closer. My back arches as pleasure erupts through me.

His fingers dip into my core, pumping in and out. He finger-fucks me with abandon. He's gentle yet rough, commanding, yet loving. My body is his to use as he pleases, and right now, he's sending me right to the edge of desire.

My stomach tightens, coils like a serpent ready to attack. His teeth graze my clit. His tongue darts into me along with two, then three fingers as I cry out his name again and again. I'm pleading, begging, crying. Tears stream down my face as I crash into nothing. My toes curl, my pussy pulsing wildly around his digits, and I gush my release on his tongue.

And like Carrick always does, he laps me up like I'm his special treat.

Twenty Three

Carrick

It's so quiet I can hear Peyton's soft breaths. She's sleeping, and I'm sitting here watching her in awe that this woman is mine. I'm planning to get her a collar as soon as possible. She needs to know that I'm not losing her again. I'm done watching her leave. It's time she stayed.

My heart started beating with Aurora, and I thought it died with her. With Peyton, she showed me that a ghost can't take a life. Peyton gave me her heart in place of mine I'd lost, and in the process, I found myself.

I've given her everything. She's all I will ever want. Soon, I want to see her pregnant with my children. I want to keep her locked up in my house while she gives me babies. It sounds so caveman. But it's true. To see her bearing my children would be a dream come true.

I want a football team. Smiling at my thoughts, I push off the bed and head into the living room. The sun is just peeking through the blinds, and I know she'll be up soon. In the kitchen, I ensure the coffee machine is on and ready to brew a pot of her favorite coffee.

The scent is heavenly when it begins to drip steadily. I watch it for a moment, lost in the hypnotic movement, I recall the confession she offered me about her own past.

This woman walked into my life one night and never left. Even those moments without her, she was never gone. She'd burrowed her way into my soul. When I didn't notice, she had ingrained herself inside me and there's no way of ever getting her out.

Not that I'd want to.

I don't hear her, she's barefoot, but I feel her.

"You're up early," she says, forcing me to turn around and devour her with my eyes. She's dressed in my white dress shirt and nothing else. Her nipples are hard beneath the material, and I'm sure her pretty pussy is wet and needy.

"I wanted to make sure you had coffee as soon as

you woke up." She smiles. Her face is angelic, but the look in her eyes is mischievous. My naughty little kitten.

"Thank you. I have so much to do today. Chance is moving to Chicago, so I need to make some space in my apartment."

"No."

"Huh?" She frowns, regarding me with confusion.

"Chance can have your apartment. You'll be living here," I tell her. There's no way she's denying me that. I want her close to me. Every damn day. And I'm not taking no for an answer. If I have to move her in myself and tie her down until she accepts it, I'll do so.

"You . . . you want me to move in here?" she questions, her big green eyes wide with shock, but she needn't feel that, because I want her here all the time. Every damn day.

"Why wouldn't I?" I stalk toward her. Gripping her hips, I pull her to me. Her body molds to mine, flush with my own. "I want to wake up and see you. I want to go to sleep at night holding you. I want to live and breathe you, Peyton Moore."

Her delicate little hands land on my chest. Her pouty

lips crack into a smile, happiness beaming from her like a beacon. My fucking lighthouse. I lift her against me, needing to feel her. Nothing like early morning sex to make my day even better.

When I pin her between the kitchen wall and my body, my fingers trail over her core. I was right -- she doesn't have panties on, and she's drenched with slick arousal.

"Always so wet for me."

"Always." Her face moves closer to mine, her lips seeking mine for a kiss, but I shake my head. Her face drops into a frown.

"I won't kiss you, Kitten, because that's not who we are. It's not what we do. But, I will make love to and fuck your perfect, pretty mouth with my own," I tell her, whispering the words over her lips. "I want our lips to mold to each other. Our tongues will dance to music only they two can hear."

She whimpers when I show her what I mean. My tongue fucks into her mouth as my cock slips into her cunt. The tight heat of her walls bears down on my cock, eliciting a growl from me.

I pull back and slam deep inside her body as if I'm part of her. "I'll use your mouth for my pleasure and yours, Kitten. Our tongues will caress each other. It will be as if two lovers are having an affair so elicit it's almost violent."

"Aren't you the poet, Sir?" She giggles, and I plunge my cock inside her again and again. Her head drops back, her nails raking over the base of my neck, my shoulders. She's being slammed into the wall by my thrusts, but she's whimpering like she's about to come. Her pussy pulses around me, attempting to milk my cock for all it's worth.

"I want you as mine, Peyton," I coo in her ear, holding her on the edge of an orgasm that will surely have her passing out. Her lips are parted in a soft moan. "For the rest of my life, I'll make love to you gently as if a butterfly's wings are touching your flesh. But I'll also fuck you hard and fast, until you're battered, bruised, and bitten with me written on your skin like a poem. Like the lyrics of your favorite song."

"Carrick, please. Oh, god," she begs as my fingers find the tight ring of muscle I'm dying to fuck as well. I tease her ass, dipping my finger into her. She's clawing at me now. Needing her orgasm, but I don't grant it.

"If you come, I'll hurt you, Kitten." She attempts to nod, but she can't. She's delirious with need. My body moves inside hers with slow thrusts. I love edging her. Big green eyes shimmer with tears. "Cry for me," I tell her.

I continue torturing her with my dick. She blinks. Her salty emotion spills down her cheeks, and I lap them up like a feral animal.

"And when I've finished using your body like it's my fuck-toy for pleasure, you'll be so wrung out on the ecstasy I'll bestow on your beautiful body, confusion will settle in your mind. You'll wonder if you need to listen to the angel or the devil that sits on either shoulder. Either guiding you to your redemption . . . or sin."

"Sir."

"And I'll be there waiting. It doesn't matter which you choose." My hips move slowly, sensually as I gently fuck her. My cock throbbing, the need to come is burning through me. "I'll be there for you. I'll be your redemption and your sin."

She opens her eyes. "May I come, Sir?" Her question has my hips moving faster. "I need you."

"Tell me, Kitten. Say the dirty words I know you love to say."

"Fuck me, Sir. Make me scream your name." I obey her. I give her what she needs. My fingers pump into her ass while my cock owns her cunt. Her arousal drips down my shaft as I piston into her. "Fuck, yes," she mumbles. Her body convulsing as I feel her walls tighten.

"Give it all to me, Peyton. Give me everything."

She does. Her orgasm strikes a match inside me as her body milks me. I empty my seed inside her, hoping with all I am that I've given her a baby.

The silence hangs around us. She doesn't move. Her head is on my shoulder. Her body limp as her legs fall down, and I know I've worn her out. My cock softens and slips from her. I walk us into the bathroom. Setting her on the counter, I take her in as she smiles when I look into her forest green eyes. They're darker here. Perhaps it's the light.

"You trying to kill me, Sir?" she sasses me playfully, and I can't help chuckling. That was one of the most intense moments of my life. The words I gave her, the way I took her, it was more than a fuck, it was more than making love. I fed her my soul, and her body accepted it willingly.

"I'd never do that. Just wanted to see how much you can take, Kitten." I wink. Grabbing a cloth, I wet it with warm water and clean her up. We should shower, but all I want to do is lie with her in my arms while the high of our orgasms subside.

"Those words. What you said . . ."

"It's true, Peyton. I'll be your sin. I'll be anything you want me to be. But I'll always ensure you're safe." She smiles. I lift her bridal-style and head into the bedroom again. Setting her down, I slip under the covers behind her and pull her against me.

"I love you, Sir."

"I love you too, Kitten."

Twenty Four

Peyton

When I woke up this morning, all I found was a note left on my pillow. He was gone before I opened my eyes, but when I took the note and sat in the kitchen, drinking the coffee he'd specially brewed knowing I'd wake up and want a mug, I read it with a smile on my face.

Kitten,

Wear the red silk dress. The one with a low back. No panties. Pink butt plug.

Your hair is to be pinned up, with strands framing your neck and face.

The jewelry you're to wear is in the vanity, a black suede box. Here's the address.

Sir

The long dress shimmers in the faded yellow light of the ballroom. Everything is draped in diamonds and gold. The room itself is opulent, with chandeliers that hang low from the high ceilings. There are cream curtains framing the windows and patio doors.

Soft music plays from the live band sitting in one corner, and the waiters and waitresses are all decked in black and white. To an outsider, this would be just another lavish party, but to those who know, this is a meeting for Dominants and submissives, Masters and slaves, and people with other kinks who frequent Seven Sins.

I move through the room taking in each face, every smile and nod. Almost in my element, I don't falter as I grab a flute of champagne from a passing tray. Sipping the bubbly liquid, I make a note of who's here.

Dresses and suits remind me of a time when things were different. My parents used to throw parties like this all the time. Waiters stroll through the room offering champagne to the guests who are elegantly dressed, more so than I am. It's utter decadence.

All Carrick's early morning requests have been

granted. I'm here, wearing exactly what he told me to. Sipping the champagne, I stroll through the crowd. Oliver is here with Chance and Leigh. Callan is with a pretty brunette. There are people I don't know, don't recognize.

Savvie and Mason are here as well, but they're performing. Putting on a rope play show for the masses. I watch for a moment, the fluidity of her body, the way Mason's hands care for her as he binds her to the hooks in the ceiling. She's weightless, like a bird.

My phone buzzes in my purse. When I take it out, I find a message from Rick.

The balcony to your left is where you'll find me.

Lifting my gaze, I find the double doors cracked open, wide enough for me to slip through. My body tingles as I walk. The plug in my ass makes me feel full, and I wonder what on earth Carrick has planned.

Even though I don't wear his ring, I know deep down we'll be together forever. Upon reaching the balcony, I find it bathed in darkness, but I don't see anyone else here. I reach the edge, my hands trembling when I set the glass down and grip the railing.

When I lean over, I take in the immaculate gardens lit by lamps all the way down a small path. I'm not sure where it leads, but I'm intrigued to find out.

"Kitten." A low, husky growl comes from behind me. When I turn, I find Rick dressed in a black tux, white dress shirt, with a black bowtie. He looks like a prince. As if he'd just stepped out of the pages of a fairytale.

"Sir." I smile. He's holding something, but I can't tell what in the low light. His approach is slow, confident. When he reaches me, he lifts his hand, his knuckles gently trailing over my cheek, leaving goose bumps in their wake.

"I've bought you something," he tells me. The box he'd been holding is small, rectangular, so I know it's not a ring. Both elation and disappointment attack me. I take it from him, lifting my gaze to his. "Open it." His voice is strained, and I wonder why.

When I snap the lid open, I find a thin silver choker with a pendant in the middle. It's cute, a small paw like shape. "This is--" I murmur. Stroking the metal, I lift it from its velvet cushion. It's only then I notice the pink gem on the paw. When I turn it over, inscribed on the pendant are the words:

Carrick's Kitten.

I snap my gaze to his in shock.

"You're mine. This means you'll always be mine. I'm collaring you, Peyton Moore. I'm devoting my time, my life, and my heart to you. All that's mine is yours."

Tears sting my eyes at his words. I swallow the lump in my throat and respond, "And all that's mine is yours. My life, my heart, and my body."

His eyes hold affection. Emotion so profound it steals my breath. The dark rings under his eyes tell me he's not been sleeping. His disheveled hair, clothes, everything about him screams broken.

He takes the choker, unfastens the clasp, and drapes it around my neck.

"You know" --he smiles, stepping back as he regards me-- "all those days without you, I had time to think. Time to relook at what I believed in. Yes, I love you. There's no doubt about that. You're the only woman in my heart right now. But, I haven't truly pushed you outside that comfort zone."

"Until tonight," I offer. He knows I'm bare under

this dress. He ordered it.

"Yes." He grips my hips, spinning me around to face the crowd, while he stands behind me in the shadows. "Lean against the railing and watch them," he orders, his body lowering behind me.

"Rick, what are you doing?" I question, but he ignores me. His hands lift the hem of my dress, his mouth blowing hot on the back of my thighs, and I realize he's about to make me come in front of everyone. Only, they can't see me. But the fact that anyone can walk out here at any moment makes my heart leap into my throat.

His hands are on me, opening the cheeks of my ass. His hot, wet tongue delves into my pussy from behind, and I can't help but whimper. He tugs and turns the plug, heightening my pleasure to unbearable levels. My body responds, my arousal soaking his fingers that are taunting me playfully.

"If you don't want them to hear you, then you'll be quiet, Kitten," he whispers over my wet core. Two fingers tease me as they stroke my slick entrance. My eyes flutter as pleasure zips through my body. My nerves crackle with electric need.

"Peyton." The rough voice of Callan O'Leary comes from the doorway, causing me to snap my eyes open. His gaze roves over me as he lights his cigarette. The cherry burns a bright red, glowing in the dark.

"I . . . Callan, I came here to be alone," I manage to mumble through the sensations of Rick's mouth suckling my pussy and his fingers dipping in and out. He pumps them faster and faster, and I know he's trying to make me come while his brother is only a few feet away.

He chuckles. "And that's why my brother is devouring your pussy?" His chin lifts in gesture toward me, but his eyes remain fixed on mine.

"I . . ." I'm not sure how to respond so I don't.

"He's always been one to push boundaries," he tells me easily as if I'm not currently having my body played with. "All the while I knew him, he didn't allow conventions to hold him back."

He doesn't make a move to leave. Instead, he nears me, leaning on the railing beside me as Carrick dips his fingers into me so deep it causes me to mewl. My hands grip onto the railing, my knuckles white with tension. Callan's eyes meet mine. They hold humor as his brother sends me to the edge.

"You sound beautiful, Peyton. You're quite the naughty girl, aren't you?" he murmurs. My knees wobble as I lean in to him. He's so close. My hands grip his shoulders, and he allows me to. He doesn't smile or acknowledge me other than staring at me as he puffs his smoke.

I'm so close. I feel the tightening in my core. Carrick must feel it too because he stops suddenly, pulling away from me. He rises behind me. "You're so delicious, Kitten," he coos in my ear as his brother calmly allows the white smoke to billow from his mouth. "Hello, Callan." Both brothers just smile. My cheeks are flushed with embarrassment as I regard both men. My gaze darting between them. "What are you doing out here?"

"Needed a smoke. Beautiful whimpers coming from her, Rick. I was eager to hear her cry out," Callan says, turning his gaze on us in amusement. My mouth drops open as I glare at him.

"Are you crazy?" I squeak in shock at his words.

"Indeed, I am." His answer holds no apology. He shrugs as if it's normal to watch your brother's girlfriend being eaten out while you have your smoke. "You see, Peyton, my brother is the good one. Me?" He leans in, inhaling me for a moment before Rick's growl behind me warns him off. "I'm the asshole who doesn't have any morals. I fuck who and when I want. I love to watch as well. Seeing a woman come is the most beautiful thing on earth, and I don't care if it's my brother, my sister, or anyone else for that matter. I enjoy a good show when I see it."

"That's enough, Cal." The warning is clear in Rick's voice. He's not impressed by his brother. Their eyes meet in a standoff, and I wonder what it is that's happened between them. "I trust you to watch, but that's it."

"Oh. I know, brother. I'm not into blondes. Besides, the pretty little senator's daughter is more than enough for me." His chuckle is dark and dangerous. He's definitely nothing like his brother. There's something violent in his eyes, and I wonder if he's into anything that Oliver is. A sadist, perhaps.

"Are you really messing with her?" Carrick questions, the frustration evident in his tone. "I told you not to piss off that family. I don't care if she wants you or not."

"I do what I want, Rick. You know that. You've always known that." The tension between the brothers skyrockets. "I'm having some fun before I leave."

"You're leaving?" The question from Carrick brings both brothers back to earth, as if the thought of not having him around makes Rick worry. Sadness seeps from him as he grips my shoulders. "I thought you'd stick around?"

"I'll think about it. Leigh is safe here with you. There's no need for me to stay." Callan drops his cigarette on the concrete and squashes it with his black boot. All the men inside, including Carrick, are dressed up, but Callan is wearing a black leather jacket, his shirt matching his charcoal eyes, and a pair of jeans I'm sure have seen better days.

He's rough around the edges. With danger in his eyes. His dark hair is disheveled. The epitome of a bad boy. And I wonder if this girl he's seeing has any inkling as to who he really is. A man who can easily end a life without a second glance.

"I'd like it if you do," Carrick says. "Come Peyton."

He pulls me along as we make our way back to the party. The men inside are all clients of Sins. They're the reason Carrick threw the party in the first place, to ensure they continue paying their membership to the club.

I learn this as we mingle with everyone. Carrick introduces me as his. I'm a possession. I smile. I shake hands, and all the while, I can't stop thinking about the life I'm about to embark on.

Epilogue

Carrick

My Kitten,

Do you recall the secrets I whisper across your flesh when you're at work? Do the moments I penned my need over your skin with my hungry tongue play on in your mind? I want you to know, every minute I'm in my office, meant to be concentrating you're on my mind. I crave one more taste, another minute to devour your poison I drink like I'm addicted.

I want to indulge in you, feast on every inch of your body until you're crying for me to stop. You offered me your virtue, you begged me to steal it with my violence with soft whimpers and moans. Your body arched, bowed toward me hungry for every touch.

As I took more and more, I wrung you dry, but still it left me thirsty. Each drop of your essence bathed me, but I wasn't pure. You weren't my salvation. You were my destruction. You broke the cold man I was and showed me the desire that burned inside, crumbling my world to ash with your innocent flames.

Now, as we walk together toward a forever, you light my way. And I'll never walk alone because even when we're old I'll still own your body, heart, mind. And you will forever own my heart and soul.

Love always,

Your Sir

I glance at the letter I've just finished writing for my woman. It's filled with emotion, with my love for her. I've allowed my heart to pour the words onto the page. And it is only for her.

My life has passed by in a dark cloud of guilt, anger, and vengeance. There was never a time I believed it would change. There are moments in life when I wished for death. When I prayed a stray bullet would finally take me from this life and deliver me to the girl I lost. My heart wasn't my own, she had taken it with her when she died.

At least . . . that's that I believed.

I spent years indulging in everything to dull the

ache of the space in my chest where my heart used to be. Each time I found another woman, I'd ensure she looked nothing like the one I lost. I made sure I was safe. From what? I don't know. I knew I couldn't fall in love again, so when I think about it now, I wonder what it is that I was hiding from.

Myself perhaps.

I drank, I fucked, and I killed.

I enjoyed it. I reveled in it.

Then I stumbled upon the blonde beauty who's currently lounging in my office on the sofa. Her legs are crossed, and on them is a MacBook Pro where she's currently doing the accounts for Seven Sins. Mason and I gave her a full-time job handling the details mainly because I can't deal with the accountants and taxes, and he is more interested in hiring and firing the staff.

Peyton slammed into my life like a goddamn wrecking ball, and she knocked every wall I built to the ground. And in that rubble, she found me. She discovered my pain and healed it. She found my heart, and instead of giving it back to me, she kept it in her hands. Those delicate hands that can tempt me to give her anything she wants as long as she teases me just right. However, that's after I've spanked her pretty ass.

"Are you going to stare at me all day?" she quips from the opposite side of the room, flicking her long, blonde waves over her shoulder. Her perfume, the scent of orchids, filters over to me, and I inhale her. She's more than perfect. She has taken to this lifestyle like a fish to water, and when she submitted to me, I was in awe of how much love I could hold for someone.

Yes, I did love Aurora, there's no doubt about that, but deep down, I now realize she was only a chapter in my story. She showed me this life didn't have to be lonely. I could commit to a woman and give her the love she deserved. And that's what I'm about to offer Peyton.

"I've been thinking," I tell her. Rising from my chair, I head over to the bar. Grabbing the chilled champagne from the cooler, I pop the cork with a loud echo. I proceed to fill two glasses, both with a strawberry dipped in chocolate floating just below the rim.

"You have? And what pray tell have you been thinking?" she taunts me, using a fake English accent to tease me. I know she loves my voice. She tells me all the time, but she does love to attempt the accent, which is done so badly I cringe.

"Well," I start, settling beside her on the sofa, handing her a flute. With one hand, I grip the laptop, setting it on the floor before turning back to her. "There's this girl," I tell her. "She's beautiful, perfect in every way, and there's something I've been wanting to ask her."

Her mouth falls open, then shuts. Her green eyes that remind me of new spring leaves shimmer and widen as she watches me. "Carrick—"

"Six months ago, I offered her a contract," I speak, clearly, confidently, but my heart rattles in my chest. "I gave her something I never thought I could give again." When I meet her gaze, she's blinked, and there's a lone tear falling down her cheek I'm tempted to lick away. "In return, she gave me something I didn't expect." Lifting the glass, I gesture for her to do the same. "Now, I want to offer her another contract. This one however . . ."

I allow my words to taper into nothing as she gapes at me.

"This one is far longer than just a four-week trial." I smirk when she blinks once more and the salty emotion trickles down her now flushed cheeks. Dropping to one knee, I take her delicate hand in mine and press a kiss to her knuckles. "Peyton Moore, will you do me the honor of accepting my ring, my collar, and ultimately, my heart?"

Her body trembles as I gulp the champagne, my eyes on her. She doesn't respond, sipping her drink slowly, but when she gets to the strawberry something just below it glitters.

"Oh god!" She gasps in shock, pulling the pink fruit from the glass. Attached to it is a five-carat diamond ring set with smaller pink diamonds surrounding it. She holds it between her thumb and forefinger, staring at it as if it's about to attack her.

I take it, pulling a napkin from my pocket and wiping it until it's dried and shiny. Holding it toward her, I take her left hand in mine. "So? Are you ready to be Mrs. Peyton O'Leary?" She nods, while tears stream down her beautiful face. "Words, Kitten. I need words."

"Yes, yes, of course yes," she mumbles while her trembling hand grips mine as if I'm her lifeline, and I plan to be. She is mine. Always has been.

I slip the ring on her finger with a smile on my face.

"Come here, wife." I pull her onto me, letting her straddle my lap. "You're so beautiful when you cry," I tell her, my hands trailing down to her ass. I squeeze, tugging her closer until her heat is right at my crotch. I'm hard. Rock fucking solid.

"I have to work." She glances back at the abandoned laptop.

"Fuck work," I bite back. Reaching for her blouse, I rip it open, buttons popping in all directions. "I'm about to make love to my wife." I lie her down. Shoving her skirt up toward her hips, I spread her thighs, finding a tiny scrap of material covering her pussy. With one harsh tug, it's on the floor, and I'm leaning in to inhale my beautiful woman's cunt.

Her slick entrance is temptation, and I'm about to indulge. My tongue darts out. Tentatively, I lick at her entrance, causing her hips to buck up toward my face. With both thumbs, I open her smooth lips and push my tongue into her. Warm, sweet juices drip from her onto my tongue, and I glance up at her big green eyes from between her thighs.

"Carrick," she utters my name, pleads, begs, tangles her fingers in my hair as I devour her sweetness. She's mine. So fucking beautifully mine. My cock is throbbing to be inside her, to just show her with my body how much I love her. I want her to come on my tongue, but I can't hold back anymore. I need to be inside her.

My slacks and boxers are around my ankles in seconds, and I'm hovering over her. My hips between her splayed thighs. "I love you, Peyton," I murmur as my cock teases her entrance. My hips roll, and I slip inside.

"I love you too, Sir," she coos, and that's all I need to drive into her body. I'm balls-deep inside the woman I'm going to marry. Leisurely, I move, sliding out and in, feeling each warm pulse of her body around my shaft.

Her fingers claw for more. She loves me being rough, fucking her, but this is not the time nor place. I need her to feel me. To feel my love. My mouth finds hers, our lips fusing with electric currents shooting through me. With each soft lick of her tongue, I offer mine in return, tasting her as she is me.

Our bodies move in sync, fitting together like two

beautiful broken pieces of the same shattered glass. We don't need anything else. No toys. No whips and cuffs. This right here is heaven. It's perfect. It's my love for Peyton, and hers for me.

Playlist

- All I Want - Jay Sean
- Lips of an Angel - Hinder
- Closer to You - Adelitas Way
- I'll Be Good - Jaymes Young
- First Time - Kygo, Ellie Goulding
- Jar of Hearts - Christina Perri
- Love Falls - HELLYEAH
- All Falls Down - Adelitas Way
- If That's Love - Shawn James
- The Shadow - Shawn James
- Lost - Anouk
- Sun on Sunday - James Blunt
- Holding My Own - The Darkness
- I Got You - Corvyx

ACKNOWLEDGMENTS

Another sin, another beautiful couple that stole my heart, and one more book that's done and dusted. Each time I hit publish, there's always an excitement that pushes me on to get to the next book. I fell in love with Carrick, yes, he's an asshole, but he just burrowed his way into my heart.

Here's your warning - Watch out for the older brother, because if you thought Rick was an asshole, Callan is going to knock that out of the water! ;)

I need to thank my BETA ladies (Cat, Allyson, Amy, Lisa, Michelle, Joy, and Caroline) for fighting over Carrick, but the clear winner was Caroline. She's claimed him so watch out, I don't think she shares. LOL!

My editor who took me on last minute, Candy, you rock lady! Thank you for making Peyton and Carrick glisten! :P

Thank you to Gabriela for taking time out of her busy schedule to proof this baby for me.

My Decadent Dolls street team who pimp me everywhere. Thank you for loving me and my books, and thank you for all your support! You ladies rock!!

My reader group, who offer an escape from everything. They keep me sane, thank you for being there to support and share laughs and even the eye candy!

To all my author colleagues, thank you for always sharing, commenting, and supporting me. I appreciate every one of you. Having a support system is important and you ladies provide that and so much more.

Readers and bloggers, from the bottom of my little black heart, THANK YOU. All you do for us authors is incredible. Reading and reviewing is demanding on your own time and you do it with a smile. Thank you so, so much. You are valued and appreciated for taking time out to show us so much love.

If you enjoyed this story, please consider leaving a review. I'd love you forever. (Even though I already do!)

SINS OF SEVEN

READ MORE ABOUT THE OTHER COUPLES IN THE SERIES

Kneel (Book #1)

Obey (Book #2)

Indulge (Book #3)

Ruthless (Book #4)

Bound (Book #5)

Envy (Book #6)

Vice (Book #7)

ABOUT DANI

Dani is a USA Today Bestselling Author of dark and deviant romance with a seductive edge.

Originally from Cape Town, South Africa, she now lives in the UK with her better half who does all the cooking while she writes all the words.

When she's not writing, she can be found binge-watching the latest TV series, or working on graphic design either for herself, or other indie authors. She enjoys reading books about handsome villains and feisty heroines, mostly dark, always seductive, and sometimes depraved.

She has a healthy addiction to tattoos, coffee, and ice cream.

www.danirene.com

info@danirene.com

FIND DANI ONLINE

Do you follow me?

If not, head over to any of the below links,

I love to hear from my readers!

Amazon - http://bit.ly/DaniAmazon

BookBub - http://bit.ly/DaniBookBub

Facebook - http://bit.ly/DaniFBPage

Facebook Group - Dani's Deviants

Goodreads - http://bit.ly/DaniGoodreads

Twitter - @danireneauthor

Pinterest - @danireneauthor

Instagram - @danireneauthor

Spotify - http://bit.ly/DaniSpotify

OTHER BOOKS

Stand Alones

Choosing the Hart

Love Beyond Words

Cuffed

Fragile Innocence

Perfectly Flawed

Black Light: Obsessed

Among Ash and Ember

Within Me (Limited Time)

Cursed in Love (collaboration with Cora Kenborn)

Beautifully Brutal (Soldati di Sangue)

How the Mind Breaks

The Devil's Plaything

While She Sleeps (Dirty Heroes Collection)

It's Never Easy (Lady Boss Press)

Only One Night (Lady Boss Press)

Deviant (Black Mountain Academy)

Taboo Novellas

Sunshine and the Stalker (collab. with K Webster)

His Temptation

Austin's Christmas Shortcake

Crime and Punishment (Newsletter Exclusive)

Tempting Grayson

Gilded Sovereign Series

Cruel War (Book #1)

Volatile Love (Book #2)

Sins of Seven Series

Kneel (Book #1)

Obey (Book #2)

Indulge (Book #3)

Ruthless (Book #4)

Bound (Book #5)

Envy (Book #6)

Vice (Book #7)

The Taken Series

Stolen

Severed

Four Fathers Series

Kingston

Four Sons Series

Brock

Carina Press Novellas

Pierced Ink

Madd Ink

Broken Series

Broken by Desire

Shattered by Love

The Backstage Series

Callum

Liam

Ryan

Forbidden Series

From the Ashes - A Prequel

Crave (Book #1)

Covet (Book #2)

Printed by Amazon Italia Logistica S.r.l.
Torrazza Piemonte (TO), Italy

38486551R00198